Cumbria
County Council
Libraries, books and more . . .

La
1.4.09

8.19 ℰ𝓌

Please return/renew this item by the last due date.
Library items may also be renewed by phone or
via our website.
www.cumbria.gov.uk/libraries

CLIC

Ask for a CLIC password

THE PLANT PROGRAMME

SUMMER LOVE

1966: When Liz Lane arrives at Rainbows Holiday Camp in Devon to work as secretary to the entertainments manager, she is thrown into a world of sand, sun and fun, despite the long hours. Her boss suspects his new secretary will be a hit with the holidaymakers, and before long Liz is wearing a Rainbows uniform. But she ends up at loggerheads with Rob, the chief host, despite their mutual attraction to each other. Will love find a way?

JILL BARRY

SUMMER LOVE

Complete and Unabridged

LINFORD
Leicester

First published in Great Britain in

2016

First Linford Edition
published 2017

Copyright © 2016 by Jill Barry

FALKIRK COUNCIL LIBRARIES

A catalogue record for this book is *available
from the British Library.*

ISBN 978–1–4448–3326–3

Published by
F. A. Thorpe (Publishing)
Anstey, Leicestershire

Set by Words & Graphics Ltd.
Anstey, Leicestershire
Printed and bound in Great Britain by
T. J. International Ltd., Padstow, Cornwall

1

It's Now or Never

Liz sucked in her breath. There it was — a long, low spread of buildings behind lofty railings. She could either ask the taxi driver to drive her straight back to the railway station, or she could pay him and walk through those gates and into her new life.

She took a half-crown from her purse and handed it to the man who'd carried her case across the pavement. 'Thank you,' she said, then hooked her handbag over one arm and looked up at the big signboard. 'Rainbows, here I come.'

'Good luck, miss.' The driver handed her a business card. 'Don't forget us any time you need a cab.'

'I won't.'

Liz took a deep breath to calm her skittish nerves and approached the man at the security kiosk. 'I have to report to the entertainments manager,' she said.

The man consulted his clipboard. 'Name, please.'

'Elizabeth Lane.' She waited, trying to appear confident.

'Ah, yes.' The official put a tick on his sheet of paper. 'If you go straight to reception over there, they'll sign you in and give you directions to your chalet. I'll let your boss know you're on your way. Good luck, love.'

'Thank you.'

He muttered something that sounded suspiciously like 'you're going to need it', but Liz pretended not to hear. She lugged her suitcase across to the reception building, pausing as she heard a whirring sound. She'd seen cinema newsreel footage of the sturdy little land trains tracking across the holiday site, carrying campers and their belongings. Maybe she could take one. Was that allowed? She had so much to learn, and she still wasn't one hundred percent sure she'd made the right decision.

She pushed the thought away as she went through the swing door. A middle-aged woman seated at a counter looked up and smiled. 'Are you Miss Lane? I heard you were on your way. You'll need to fill in a form, and then we'll get you to your quarters. Mr Boyd's anxious to see you as soon as possible.'

'Oh, dear,' said Liz. 'I haven't a clue where anywhere is.'

'Don't you worry, I'll give you a plan of the camp layout.' She handed a sheet of paper to Liz. 'Basically it's divided into four areas — North, South, East and West. You're in West Blue. Your chalet mate's a Rainbow hostess, but I doubt you'll meet her yet. I hope you have plenty of stamina, Miss Lane.'

Liz stared back at her in horror.

'Anyway, here's your key. Be sure not to lose it, especially after 8.00 p.m. when we close reception.'

*   *   *

Liz, suitcase stowed in the baggage truck at the rear of the blue-painted train, gazed around her as the driver threaded his way across the camp. She noted signs pointing to dining halls, to the children's crèche, and to the chapel and quiet area. The driver stopped several times, once opposite a large building with a signboard saying 'entertainments' on it. At one end was the theatre, and at the other were a caféteria and a bingo hall. Presumably the office where she'd work was located on the top floor. She gazed up at the row of windows and spotted another sign telling her this was the home of Rainbow Radio.

Liz waved back at a clown dressed in scarlet waistcoat, baggy white shirt and black and white chequered trousers. He stood beside a family, and Liz turned round to watch him keep blinking and rubbing his eyes, insisting he must be seeing double. The parents watched, smiling, as their little twin girls, their hair in bunches, their faces shining with joy, giggled and pointed to the clown's giant shiny boots.

At West Blue, the friendly driver handed Liz her case and, like the gatekeeper, wished her good luck. She longed for a cup of tea but creating a good first impression seemed more important. Inside her new summer home she saw two single beds, one either side of the chalet, each made up with a blue counterpane and snow-white linen. One bed resembled that of Liz's teenage brother. A teddy bear squinted at her from the pillow, and among the tangled sheets were a couple of magazines, a hairbrush and a half-eaten chocolate bar. Liz plonked down her case on the unused bed and pulled out her toilet bag. After a quick wash and tidy-up, she'd walk to the entertainments centre.

But outside she hesitated, uncertain which way she should go. This section housed staff members, so signboards were like hens' teeth, as her dad would say and there was no sign of a camp train. She strode to the end of her block and peered left and right where, a few yards away, she saw two young men, each wearing the blue blazer and white trousers of a Rainbow host. They were with a group of holidaymakers who appeared to be hanging on every word.

As she approached, one of the Rainbows turned and smiled at her. 'You have to be a candidate for the Miss Style contest! If you are, then come with us.'

Liz laughed. 'You're wrong, I'm afraid.'

He pulled a sad face. 'Forgive me for being so bold, but we could do with a few more blondes. Won't you consider entering?'

'Sorry, but I'm new, and my boss is waiting for me. Could you direct me to the entertainments centre please, um . . . ' She noticed the young man's name badge. 'Colin?'

'We're going that way. Are you a new Rainbow?'

'No, I'm a secretary, and my name's Liz Lane.'

'Does that mean you're replacing Sadie?'

'I've no idea, but I'm here to work for Mr Boyd.'

Colin nodded. 'Stuart's been tearing his hair out. The fair Sadie eloped with one of the Rainbows last week.'

Liz gasped. 'So that's why he's so anxious for me to start work!'

'You bet your life. Mind you, Sadie often couldn't get the daily schedule right, though I imagine preparing that's a bit like doing a thousand-word jigsaw puzzle. How's your typing?'

Liz swallowed. 'Not too bad.' She wondered what she was letting herself in for. But working for the entertainments manager surely couldn't be more difficult than acting as the right-hand woman to an engineer and being expected to decipher his handwritten quotations. Translating her former employer's scribbles into technical terms like joists or stanchions had taken her ages to become accustomed to. The words 'double Dutch' came to mind. Was she about to exchange one tortuous task for another?

Liz's stomach lurched. She was an

experienced secretary with a glowing reference from an employer who was sorry to see her go. So why did she suddenly want to turn round and go home again?

Colin stopped to sign a young lad's autograph book. Liz looked enquiringly at him as the boy ran across to the other Rainbow host. 'I'm sorry, Colin, but should I recognise you?' She knew that many entertainers applied for jobs as Rainbow hosts or hostesses, hoping to be discovered and given the chance to start climbing the wobbly rope ladder to the stars.

Colin chuckled. 'Nope. You'll see lots of the kids asking us for our autographs. It's a bit of a thing with them.'

'Maybe they hope one of you'll become a pop star one day.'

'I sing like a corn crake, so it won't be me! I'm honing my swimming coach credentials.' He stopped again and gestured to the building looming ahead. 'There's where you need to be. Walk through the café, go up the stairs, and you'll find the entertainments offices on the first floor. We need to be Jacks or Jills of all trades here, when push comes to shove, so one of the girls has been doing her best to keep things going.'

Liz reminded herself she'd wanted a challenge and managed a little smile.

'Go into the secretary's office first, and Jenny will let you know if the boss is free. I wouldn't mind betting Stuart jumps for joy when he claps eyes on you.'

★   ★   ★

'Come in.' The voice sounded pleasant, deep and tinged with a touch of tartan. Liz pushed open her new boss's door.

The tall man seated at a cluttered desk in front of the window jumped to his feet and held out his hand. 'Miss Lane? Thank goodness! I'm Stuart Boyd. Now tell me, do I call you Elizabeth?'

His expression was a little harassed, though Liz found his friendly tone encouraging. 'Being called Elizabeth makes me feel like I'm back at school, or in trouble with my mother!'

He nodded, his attention focused on her.

'So if it's all right with you, Liz is how I'm usually known.'

'Excellent — and I appreciate you coming to see me so quickly. I only wish I didn't have to throw you in at the deep end, Liz.'

She sat down and clasped her hands on top of her handbag. 'One of the Rainbows told me to call at the secretary's office first. He said one of the ladies was helping out.'

'That's right, but only for a few hours each day. She's been doing her best, but I need a trained secretary like you. Someone used to fielding calls and making decisions. Jenny's fabulous with the kiddies, and she can type, but she can't do shorthand.'

'But she could at least show me the ropes?'

Stuart Boyd shrugged. 'Basic things,

yes, if you think that's necessary.'

For a moment, Liz detected a flash of amusement in his eyes. 'It's a very different environment from my last position, Mr Boyd, but I'm looking forward to learning all about the entertainments business.'

'I got a copy of your last employer's reference in the post this morning. Sounds like they were sorry to see you go. A touch of efficiency wouldn't go amiss here, Miss — erm — Liz.'

Liz looked him in the eye. 'I'll do my best, Mr Boyd.'

'I'm sure you will. Anything less like a well-functioning office, I've yet to see.'

Her heart sank. Hopefully he was exaggerating. There seemed to be several veiled warnings coming her way.

Stuart Boyd glanced at his watch. 'I'm due to watch a new act audition at the theatre. Grab yourself a notebook and pen from next door and meet me downstairs in ten minutes. You might as well see what you've let yourself in for.'

He picked up the phone.

Liz considered herself dismissed.

'Russ? We're all looking forward to your visit, old chap,' said her new boss.

She closed the door quietly behind her. No, surely he couldn't be speaking to Russ Hamilton! Could he? After all, many people knew the singer had begun his career working for a rival holiday organisation, and the Rainbow camps were also known for their high standard of entertainers.

Next door, Jenny, the pretty redhead Liz had met briefly only minutes before, was rubbing at the paper in her machine with a typing eraser. She looked up at Liz and sighed. 'Don't you just hate it when you make a mistake and you've got a top sheet and four carbon copies?'

'Couldn't agree more,' said Liz. 'But you'll be pleased to hear Mr Boyd hasn't sent me packing yet. So you're off the hook as soon as you've given me a bit of instruction.'

Jenny beamed. 'That's the best thing

I've heard since personnel dragged me in here. In my humble opinion, they should find you an assistant.'

'How did they cope when Sadie took a day off? There are entertainments taking place throughout the week, aren't there?'

Jenny nodded. 'Angie used to help out, but now she's in charge of Rainbow Radio, so she really can't do that anymore. There's a detailed schedule put together each day by the chief Rainbow — his name's Rob Douglas. It'll be your job to type it up and make sure there are no clashes. And Rob always wrote out the schedule by hand on Sadie's day off, so maybe he'll carry on doing that.'

Liz concentrated, scribbling reminders on a lined notepad Jenny pushed towards her, until a glance at her watch sent her shooting to her feet. 'I'd better go. Mr Boyd said he'd see me downstairs.'

'Whoops, sorry, I should've remembered that audition. See you later, and we'll grab a coffee. I gather they've put you in the same chalet as me.'

Liz looked at a desk rivalling Stuart Boyd's in untidiness. Some things would have to change around here. But she'd taken an immediate liking to her new chalet mate, even if she thrived on chaos.

'I'll be here until it's time to go to the evening meal,' said Jenny. 'I guess they've allocated you to the first sitting?'

Liz nodded. 'Does that mean I finish for the day then?'

'In theory it does. You're not a Rainbow, so you should follow normal office hours.' She paused. 'Not that anything's truly normal around here.'

'Okay. I'd better get a move on.'

She clattered down the stairs to find her new boss waiting at the bottom of the flight.

'I'm so sorry. Jenny's been giving me a briefing.'

He rolled his eyes. 'Ach, she does her best. Let's get on, Liz. I've asked the

14

theatre manager's secretary to fetch us a cup of tea. Is that all right?'

'Mr Boyd, I would give anything for a cuppa,' said Liz, following behind as he strode to the door.

'We're lucky having our offices above the café,' he said over his shoulder. 'I don't mind you taking a couple of short breaks during office hours, and we need to decide on your day off, though it'd be helpful if you were flexible as to which day.'

Liz nodded. 'What happens if you're away from the office and I'm on my own?'

'People will ring back if they really want to contact me. We could do with an admin assistant, but I can't promise that's going to happen.'

They walked along to the Rainbow's End Theatre, and Liz found herself in a foyer that was red-carpeted with gilt pillars. Stuart Boyd strode over to the box office and spoke to the clerk.

'We're okay to go through.' He headed for the doors through to the stalls, suddenly whirling round to face Liz. 'While I remember, you're welcome to watch any of the shows, provided you're not taking up a seat and preventing a guest from using it. No seats can be booked in advance, except very occasionally in the case of VIPs. Every single holidaymaker is entitled to free entertainment on site.'

'Thank you,' she said. 'That sounds wonderful.' She was addressing her boss's back.

He pushed open the swing doors, Liz trotting behind, still clutching her notepad. She followed him down the red-carpeted aisle, row by row, until they reached the front.

'If you take a seat in the front row,' said Mr Boyd, 'I'll sit behind you; and if I need you to jot down comments, I'll let you know.'

'Two teas!' A grey-haired woman wearing a navy linen shift dress appeared as if from nowhere.

'That's very kind, Miriam,' said Mr Boyd.

'What a life-saver.' Liz accepted her china mug gratefully.

'Wasn't sure about sugar for you, Miss Lane. Your boss takes it by the ton, of course.'

'Three lumps is hardly unusual,' said Mr Boyd, looking hurt.

Liz shook her head as Miriam held out a small plastic beaker. 'Not for me, thanks.'

'No wonder you have a figure like that!'

Liz was pleased Stuart Boyd was on the move again, this time his attention focused on the orchestra pit where three or four men carrying musical instruments were taking their places. Another sat down at the piano.

'Sorry, I meant that as a compliment.' Miriam made a face at Liz. 'Looking at you, I'm surprised Stuart hasn't decided to put you in uniform by now.'

'Me? I only just got here and I'm a secretary, not a hostess.'

'Hmm.' Miriam winked. 'Bet you

sixpence you'll be wearing a Rainbow outfit by the end of the week. Just you wait and see.' She glanced up at the stage. 'Here come the boys.'

'What kind of act is it?'

'They're Irish folk singers, and two of them do a bit of clog dancing while the other two fiddle.'

'Right,' said Liz. Her new job might be tricky to get the hang of, but it looked as if there wouldn't be too many dull moments. She'd come a very long way from chassis specifications.

When the musicians played the opening toe-tapping notes, Liz reminded herself she'd better keep still when her new boss found something he needed jotting down. She might sometimes wonder whether she was still in the real world or not, but already she was enjoying herself.

Yet, by the end of the afternoon Liz longed to change into shorts and a sleeveless top and walk down to the beach.

'You must be tired after your train journey,' said Jenny. 'Why don't you give your parents a ring and let them know you've arrived safe and sound? Then you can get something to eat and do some exploring if you want.'

'I'd love to go to the beach, if that's allowed.'

Jenny laughed. 'Contrary to what you might hear people say in the town, Rainbows isn't a prison.'

'Is that really what people say?'

'I think it's because the holidaymakers truly don't need to leave the camp if they don't want to. But don't try coming back after midnight, because the gates close then and the security people don't open them again until six in the morning.'

'I doubt I'll be tempted to stay out till that time, but thanks for the tip, Jenny.'

'Now make that phone call before Rainbow Radio summons you to the dining hall!'

'Okay, but I wouldn't want Mr Boyd to think I was taking advantage on my very first day.'

'He'd expect you to ring home, Liz. He's got a family of his own, strange as it may seem.'

Liz raised her eyebrows.

'I meant the poor souls don't see too much of him. Fortunately he has a house not far away, so the children visit the camp sometimes. His kids love it, of course.'

Liz dialled her home number, swallowing a lump in her throat when her mother answered at the second ring.

'I hoped it might be you, love.'

'I'm ringing from the office, Mum, so it's just a quick word to let you know the journey was fine.'

'That's good. Accommodation all right?'

'I've hardly spent five minutes in my chalet but I'm sharing with a nice girl.'

'Do you think you'll like working there? I still don't understand why you gave up a steady job for one that'll finish at the end of September.'

Liz had heard this several times before and wasn't sure how to answer, but opted to stay positive. 'The first few days in any new job are always tough, Mum. My boss seems a real live wire, but then he has to be, don't you think?'

'I expect so, Lizzie.' Her mother sounded doubtful. 'Oh — your dad's gone to the allotment, but he said to send his love if you should ring.'

'Send mine back to him. I'll buy a postcard to pop in the post as soon as I can. And tell that little brother of mine he'd love it here. There are so many things to do.'

'We'll have to see how you get on, then. Maybe we could bring Richard and all spend a week a bit later in the season.'

'That'd be great. I imagine the school hols are pretty well booked up, but let me find my feet and I'll see what I can find out.'

'Richard wants to know if you've managed to visit the beach yet.'

'Tell him I might get a walk in after I've eaten.'

'You mind where you go when you're

away from the camp. Oh Lizzie, we'll all miss you, but it sounds as if you're going to be too busy to be homesick.'

'That's a good thing, isn't it?'

'I can't argue with that, love.'

Liz said her goodbyes and put the phone down thoughtfully. Her new job was a different country compared with her former one. She'd longed for a change of career and of scenery, and now here she was, miles from home, in a world that, if not crazy, revolved around families having fun rather than keeping engines running. Her head might be whirling after she completed typing the next day's events schedule, but she doubted boredom would ever be a problem at Rainbows.

When Jenny returned, she couldn't believe Liz had already finished her typing task. 'How can anybody type so fast? You should be in *The Guinness Book of Records*, Liz!'

'I don't think so! You'd better check it for me, Jenny, please. I'd hate there to be any mistakes.'

'I promise I will, but you must go to the dining room now. It's almost six o'clock. I should sit where you like this evening, but I imagine they'll allocate you a table tomorrow.'

'You and I aren't allowed to eat together, I suppose?'

'I'm on the second sitting. First breakfast starts at seven fifteen, but as long as you're in the office by eight thirty, you'll be all right. I'll see you back at the chalet, but I won't turn up until eleven or so.'

'Goodness, how do you cope with such long hours?'

'I've been working split shifts since Sadie ran off. I miss being with the children, though.'

'When do you think they'll let you return to your normal duties?'

Jenny laughed. 'Tomorrow! I'm afraid you're on your own from then on.'

2

Don't Think Twice, It's All Right

Next morning Liz was roused from slumber by the voice of Gordon MacRae singing 'Oh What a Beautiful Morning'. This was one of her mother's favourite songs, and at first Liz wondered where on earth she was and why a radio was playing in her bedroom. It didn't take long for the events of the previous day to come flooding back.

She lifted her head and looked across at the bed opposite. Amazingly, Jenny still slept, her coppery hair spread across the white pillow. Liz hadn't made it to the beach last night. She'd enjoyed her meal and chatted with a pleasant family from Pembrokeshire, and afterwards she'd walked to the café in the entertainments centre for a comforting chocolatey drink before heading back to the chalet. She'd barely kept awake long enough to unpack her case and brush her teeth before crashing into bed, and had no recollection of her chalet mate coming in. Now it looked as though Jenny was going to sleep through Liz's preparation for a day at the office.

She was dressed and ready to leave when Jenny propped her head on an elbow, yawned and wished her a good morning.

'Good morning to you too,' said Liz. 'How on earth did you manage to sleep through that wake-up call?'

'Years of practice. This is my third summer working here, remember?'

'I do now! Goodness, I slept well.' Liz checked her watch. 'I'd better be off.'

Jenny struggled to a sitting position. 'Have a good day, Liz. I'm sure you'll be fine. You're obviously an experienced secretary.'

'Trouble is, Jenny, I have a feeling my

previous office job isn't going to be much help in this one.'

'But you're a fast typist, and you can read back your own shorthand.'

'Hopefully!'

'I'll call in later, but I doubt anything's going to faze you. I like your frock, by the way. Those big pink spots are very fashionable.'

'Thank you. I used to wear lots of navy blue and dark grey in my last job, so I almost feel like I'm on holiday here.'

'Let's hope that feeling doesn't wear off too soon, then. Ta-ta for now.'

Liz let herself out into another sunny morning. Other employees were appearing from their chalets. Most of the Rainbow hosts and hostesses seemed to be clustered at her end of the block. This was a culture she'd never before experienced. She couldn't help feeling overawed by the sight of so many people dressed in the iconic uniform she'd seen in newsreels at the cinema and at home on TV over the years. Her young brother would be thrilled to bits.

A curly-haired young man in his blue-and-whites emerged through the door of a chalet just ahead and clattered down the short flight of steps onto the walkway.

'Good morning.' He stopped and peered at her name badge. 'Hello, Liz.' He raised his eyebrows. 'So you're on the staff? At first I thought you must be a holidaymaker who'd taken a wrong turn.'

She read his name badge. 'Good morning. Are you by any chance Rob Douglas?'

'Not if you're a private investigator,' he said, sneaking a sly glance over his shoulder.

Her lips twitched. 'Ah, you're obviously the camp comic.'

He groaned. 'The truth is out, but yes, for my sins I'm Rob Douglas. How long have you been working here, then?'

'I started yesterday, so I'm very much the new girl, though Jenny's been great helping me settle in.'

'I guess that must mean you're Stuart's new secretary. I had to go to London yesterday, so I didn't realise he'd already found a replacement. Maybe we'll see a smile on his face more often, now you've arrived.'

Liz grimaced. 'Unless I make a mess of the next schedule. That's always possible.'

'The one I have in my pocket is first class. Did you type it?'

'I did. Jenny was going to check it for me, as I had to go to first-sitting dinner.'

Liz noticed Rob had cut his long stride so that she could keep in step with him. 'How many summers have you worked here, Rob?'

'One more than Jenny, which makes four.' He smiled down at her. 'Some of us are gluttons for punishment, aren't we?'

'It's not hard to understand why you enjoy your life, but you all work such long hours. And what happens to you at the end of the season?'

As they left the staff accommodation

area, Liz noticed holidaymakers stream-
ing down the main concourse towards
the dining hall, most of them looking
very cheerful.

Rob waved at a group. 'They're on
my table,' he said, leaving her query
unanswered. 'I'm sorry I can't sit with
you so we can become better acquainted.
You must have lots of questions.'

'That's all right,' she said. It was his
job to be friendly, and he couldn't possibly mean he wanted to know her better.
'I understand hosts and hostesses must
mingle with the holidaymakers.'

'But as you're in civvies, we might
just get away with you sitting next to
me this morning.'

'Really, it's fine, Rob, thanks. I'll sit
anywhere there's a space. Best I don't
get a telling-off on my first day going it
alone in the office.'

'All right, but I'm very glad you're
joining the entertainments team. I'm in
and out of the office a lot, so you'll be
fed up with the sight of my ugly mug
before too much longer.'

She rather doubted that but didn't dare tell him. The Rainbows chief was probably used to teenagers and grannies worshipping him. No surprise, given his dark good looks.

'You really should be allocated a table, not have to find a place every meal time. Hang on.' Rob held the door open for her. 'I'll just ask.'

Liz opened her mouth to protest but closed it again as he strode towards the service area. She saw him speak to a man wearing catering whites, and after a brief conversation Rob returned, a wide smile on his face.

'The supervisor says you can have a place at the table across from mine. There's no Rainbow at that one, since Sadie and Jim ran away to sea.'

'Ran away to sea?'

'Joking! In fact, it might be that I'm not joking at all, because the word is they'd both applied for jobs on a cruise liner. Goodness knows how they pulled that off without asking Stuart for a reference.' He pulled out a chair at the head of a table. 'Here you go. You can be table prefect. Enjoy your breakfast, Liz. Mornin', everybody.'

He moved away, bestowing smiles in all directions as he acknowledged a chorus of greetings. How on earth did he do that all day? Liz sat down hurriedly, smiling shyly at the people already seated.

'Hello me duck,' said a woman sitting two places away. 'New, are you? I can't read your name badge without my glasses.'

'I'm Liz.'

'What brings you here, my love? Are you going to be a Rainbow?'

'I'm afraid not. I'm a secretary and I fancied a change of routine.'

'Well, you've come to the right place, I reckon.' The woman smiled up at the waitress putting a plate of sausage, egg and bacon in front of her.

Liz ordered orange juice and scrambled eggs on toast. Suddenly she felt peckish, though she couldn't wait to get across to the office and start to get the feel of her new job.

Walking from the dining hall to the entertainments centre gave her a buzz. Her journey to her previous job had involved a ten-minute walk to the bus stop and a commute of twenty minutes chugging through traffic, followed by a short walk to the firm's premises. Here, there were no exhaust fumes and no blaring car horns. People strolled. Children scooted. Tots skipped. Smiling mums in pretty cotton dresses guided pushchairs down the wide walkways. Dads dressed in casual shirts and trousers or shorts looked relaxed and relieved not to be part of the rush and bustle of everyday life. And wherever you went, there was a pleasant young man or woman wearing the distinctive blazer of the host or hostess in one of the four colours: pink, blue, yellow, or green.

'Where have you been all my life, darling?'

Startled, Liz turned round to find herself face to face with a round-faced man dressed in a green blazer, white shirt and green trousers. He wore a jaunty bow tie instead of the conventional one worn by the other male Rainbow hosts she'd seen. He also seemed older than most, maybe in his late thirties. His black hair was slicked down and he had a small moustache, giving him the air of an old-time film star. She didn't know quite how to respond. There seemed to be a new experience around every corner, but she had to become accustomed to her new surroundings.

'Wherever you've been, you're here now,' he said, holding out his hand. 'Harry Barnes, resident comedian.'

She shook hands. 'I'm Liz Lane, trying my best to pretend I understand what's going on in the entertainments office.'

His eyes were kindly. 'So you're the lovely blonde some of the boys were talking about last night. I must say, you look a picture in that dress.'

Liz blinked hard. 'I don't know about that.'

'News travels fast round here. Tell me, before you slip away into Stuart's clutches, do you sing, Liz? Dance? Juggle? Impersonate Shirley Bassey?'

He looked so hopeful! Liz burst out laughing. 'Sorry, but I only sing in the bath. I went to ballet classes when I was a child, but the only dancing I've done recently has been on Saturday nights at the local hop.'

'You should enjoy the dances here, then. Our resident instructors, Mick and Helen, run classes most mornings, and the orchestra's on the go every evening in the Buckingham Ballroom.'

Liz laughed. 'I don't think Mr Boyd's going to give me time off for dancing lessons. I don't want to seem rude, Harry, but there's a mountain of work waiting, so if you'll excuse me . . . '

Harry nodded. 'Of course. I'm sure you'll cope beautifully, Miss Liz Lane. If you don't mind me offering a bit of advice, it's often best not to think twice once you've made a decision. Life moves fast here, but I think everything's going to be all right. Trust me, I'm a Rainbow.'

She laughed. 'Okay, and thanks for your kind words.'

'I'll pop in and say hello next time the boss calls me into one of his meetings, but I have a feeling you'll fit in very well.'

Liz hurried up the stairs to the administration floor. Harry had been very welcoming, but he'd reminded her of something when he mentioned meetings. She must make sure Mr Boyd had everything he needed in the way of background information, phone numbers and so on. She found her office unlocked, but when she tapped on his door there was no response. She collected her notebook and pencil, went into his room and stood, gazing at the chaos on his desk.

'I know. It's awful, isn't it?'

She turned to face Stuart Boyd leaning in the doorway, arms folded. 'I — I do wonder how you find things.'

'To be truthful, I often can't. But you have enough to do without tidying up after me.'

'What you need is a couple of wire trays. I could go down to the stationery room if you give me a chit. Then I can sort out any invoices awaiting approval and letters needing urgent attention. How does that sound?'

At last she'd raised a smile. 'It sounds just fine,' he said.

'I wonder if I could borrow your diary so I can copy your appointments into mine. That way I can do any research that might be necessary.'

He blinked rapidly. 'My diary? Now, I wonder where I left it.'

Liz longed to dive into the muddle, but luckily she spotted a book with a black cover. She leaned across and picked it up.

He took the diary from her with a sheepish grin. 'Let's see now — meeting at eleven with a couple of the town councillors. They'll need collecting from reception. Could you do that?'

She nodded. 'Should I bring them here?'

'Good question.' He eyed his desk.

'As there's only two of them, we could use that small room off Rainbow Radio. If you could check there are three chairs? Tell Angie I sent you.'

'I haven't met the presenter yet. She was busy with announcements when Jenny put her head round the studio door yesterday.'

'Oh dear, I didn't realise you and Angie hadn't met.'

'She has a lovely voice, don't you think? Whoops, I suppose you appointed her, so you must think so!'

'I'm also married to her.'

Liz gasped. 'Gosh, I'm sorry. I didn't realise.'

He looked at her, head to one side. 'Come to think of it, you speak nicely too. I must ask Angie if she'll train you so you can stand in for the odd hour. My mother-in-law helps with the children, but if you're happy to learn your way around the equipment, that would be very useful. Angie has a couple of stand-ins, but we could definitely do with someone like you.'

Liz's stomach lurched. There were more wobbly-stomach moments here than she'd experienced anywhere else, including school, where she had faced a constant battle with the torturous contraptions in the gymnasium. Despite her protests, her PE teacher had refused to accept Liz just wasn't built for somersaults or vaulting over a bolster on stilts.

'And I really do mean it when I say I'm hoping to get approval to take on a part-timer. Someone from the town would be ideal.'

She nodded. 'There's a lot to do, but I'm sure I can make inroads.'

'We'll have a chat later. Now, I need to dictate an urgent memo, then I'll leave you to get on.'

Stuart reeled off a couple of paragraphs, then turned around and clattered off down the stairs. Liz wasn't sure whether to be doubtful or delighted by her boss's confidence that she knew what she was doing.

★   ★   ★

Not long before lunch, a tall, slender, pretty woman with long dark hair appeared in Liz's doorway. 'You look very calm,' she said. 'Angie told me you only started work yesterday.' She held out her hand. 'I'm Cathy from the dance troupe.'

'Pleased to meet you,' said Liz. 'You're the head girl, aren't you?'

Cathy smiled. 'Yes, but only since last week when the original one left unexpectedly.'

'Goodness,' said Liz. 'No wonder Mr Boyd looks harassed most of the time.' She clapped her hand to her mouth. 'I shouldn't have said that! Personal secretaries should always be discreet.'

Cathy shook her head. 'Don't worry. The poor man's had two employees leave in a short space of time. It's a hard enough job anyway, juggling all us lot, as no doubt you're fast finding out.' Her dark eyes sparkled with merriment.

'So you and I are both new girls in a way,' said Liz.

'That's right. Fortunately, I was

already standing in as head girl a fair bit, so it's not as tough as it might've been. We have a special routine head office want us to practise, so my work's cut out at the moment.'

'Is that just for here, or does it apply to all the camps?' Liz was keen to learn more about the organisation.

'Certain routines are standard at all the camps, but we do have some choice as to what we perform. How about you, Liz? Have you worked at a Rainbow camp before?'

'Far from it. After my secretarial course, I went to work for a local construction company and got promoted to managing director's secretary two years ago.'

'Well done,' said Cathy.

'The salary increase was very welcome, but I got fed up with all those technical terms and long quotations I had to type.'

'They must've thought a lot of you, but what made you apply for a job here?'

'I wanted a complete change.'

'Well, you've certainly achieved that.'

Liz laughed. 'So everyone says! I wrote to head office earlier this year but heard nothing. Mr Boyd's phone call came out of the blue, and before I knew it I'd agreed to work for him. So I didn't even have an interview. I don't think my mother's recovered from the shock yet!'

'Let's hope you don't find being here too shocking. I love dancing and enter-taining people, but it's not all roses, as you can imagine.'

'I imagine it means lots of practising and hard work. I hope I can watch you perform some time.'

'I'm sure you will. There are twelve of us dancers, and we also carry out hostess duties, though you wouldn't recognise our names on the schedule.'

'Everyone works such long hours! What happens if a dancer is ill?'

'One or two hostesses are able to stand in. but fingers crossed, that doesn't happen very often!' She hesitated. 'Don't let anyone take advantage of you, Liz. Remember what they say about the willing horse? You need your time off.' She glanced at her watch. 'I'm due at rehearsal, but maybe we can have coffee together some time?'

'I'd like that.' Liz felt a little surge of warmth. Cathy was so glamorous, so friendly, and probably had many fascinating stories to tell about her dancing career.

Left enjoying a drift of whatever gorgeous perfume the dancer used, Liz turned her attention back to her notebook. Cathy's words of warning were doubtless well-meant, but could long and unpredictable hours have been the reason for her predecessor leaving so suddenly with her Rainbow boyfriend?

She pushed her thoughts away, fingers flying as she typed. After she'd escorted Mr Boyd's visitors from reception and into the small meeting room, she hurried downstairs again and bought coffees to take into the meeting.

On her way back, the radio presenter beckoned to her. Liz opened the door carefully and stepped inside.

'It's okay,' said Angie. 'I'm playing three discs one after another so we can talk. How's it going, Liz? I hope that husband of mine's not working you too hard.'

'At the moment I feel as if I need water wings. There's so much to learn, but I'm enjoying it.'

'Well, Stuart came home last night and told me how relieved he was to have someone competent helping him. Believe me, that's high praise from him.'

'Let's hope he feels the same by this time next week!' Liz grinned. 'I don't know how you cope with this job as well as bringing up a family and running a household. My mum stopped working in a shop when she got married and she's still a full-time homemaker.'

'I'm lucky my mum's able to help me with the children. Stuart's hours are, of course, a nightmare, but he loves his job.'

'I mustn't stay long,' said Liz. 'But how long has he been entertainments manager?'

'This is only his second year. We were in Scotland before.'

'That's quite a distance from here. How are you liking this area?'

'We love it. My mother's widowed, so she was pleased to move with us; she has a little bungalow not too far from our house. Neither of our two boys was at school before we moved, so that was one thing we didn't have to worry about. They've settled in well, thank goodness.'

'That's good. Maybe I'll meet them one of these days.'

'They'd take over my job if they could! You have been warned.'

Liz let herself out. Angie hadn't mentioned training her, but the number of knobs and switches on the control console looked a bit too complex for Liz's liking. Maybe it would all come to nothing. It wasn't as if she hadn't enough to do already, and she certainly didn't intend to remind her boss of his suggestion.

3

I Get Around

Liz hardly saw her chalet mate unless it was first thing in the morning or last thing at night. One day melted into the next, and still she hadn't got to the beach. After a week in her new job, she decided the time had arrived to remind her boss they hadn't fixed which day she should take off.

She waited until he'd finished dictating letters and memos and got a surprise when he complimented her on fitting in so well.

'Thank you, Mr Boyd,' she said. 'I'm enjoying the work, but it would be good to have some time away from the office — only when it's convenient, of course.'

He peered at her over the top of the horn-rimmed spectacles she'd noticed he wore when having to stretch his attention span. 'Oh dear, I'm so pleased you spoke up. How long have you been working for me now, Liz?'

'This is the eighth full day.'

He groaned and riffled through one of his new trays. 'I received something from personnel — ah, here it is.' He scanned the memo and handed it across the desk. 'How about you take tomorrow off, Liz? But from next week on, perhaps Tuesday would be the best day. We'll get Jenny to spend time in the office when you're off duty.'

Liz nodded but daren't ask if there was any hope of a clerical assistant being taken on. 'Thank you.'

'And while I think of it, I'd like you to wear blue and white. Give personnel a ring and tell them I want you to be kitted out with two uniforms.'

'Two?'

'One on and one in the laundry. That's what everyone has.'

'Well, if that's what you think best. Me going into uniform, I mean.'

Already he was reaching for the

phone. 'Thanks, Liz.'

On the way back to her office, she could hear faint strains of the music being played by Rainbow Radio. 'I Get Around' seemed very appropriate at the moment. She was already loving her job, especially enjoying checking the schedule to remind her where to find a particular host or hostess, whenever Stuart Boyd had an instruction. Liz loved these brief glimpses at whatever activity was going on.

'Angie's stuck inside her studio, of course, so she doesn't have too much opportunity to visit venues. I want you to carry out spot checks, Liz, and report back to me if something seems amiss.' That was what her boss had said, and that was what she was doing, although at first she'd felt as though she was spying.

⋆ ⋆ ⋆

That evening, knowing she had the next day to herself, Liz ate in the dining hall before wandering along to the camp theatre. Arriving to find the seats filling up with chattering holidaymakers was a very different experience from her first visit to take notes at the audition. She confirmed with the box office that there were spare places before slipping into an end seat on a row towards the rear of the auditorium.

Harry the resident comic was already on stage, doing his warm-up before the show began. He looked, thought Liz, very much at ease.

'There's a gentleman who's booked in for a holiday this week and his name is Mr Dracula.' He waited for the ripple of laughter to subside. 'But sadly he's finding it difficult to make friends.' Harry paused again. 'I reckon it's because he's such a pain in the neck!'

The appalling joke was greeted with groans but laughter too. Liz decided the comedian possessed excellent timing, and the crowd were enjoying the quips and banter between Harry and a Rainbow hostess in yellow and white who stood near the front, making sure people were finding seats together and helping the less mobile holidaymakers negotiate the wide carpeted steps.

Harry left the stage to applause. The dark red curtains swished apart and the orchestra began playing the introduction to a catchy tune Liz recognised as 'The African Waltz'. The troupe of dancing girls ran on stage, formed a line and began their routine. Liz couldn't stop herself nodding to the beat as they dipped and sashayed in perfect unison. Cathy, the head girl, was at one end of the line; she, like the others, was wearing a long-sleeved silky pink top with a flared skirt that, when she moved, whirled and swirled in a sunburst of colours.

The girls gained noisy applause and went straight into another number, this time Del Shannon's 'Runaway'. A guitarist came on stage and performed a rip-roaring solo that had some audience members bouncing up and down in their seats. The enthusiastic response at the end was even greater than before.

Then Harry was back. This time he sang 'The Naughty Lady of Shady Lane', and Liz realised what a lovely warm voice he had. He also knew how to put a song over.

The melody was just ending when a man dressed as a woman, wearing a pair of high-heeled shoes, tip-tapped onto the stage and fluttered a pair of huge false eyelashes at Harry. The comic chased away this intruder, but the outrageous dame returned with the dancing troupe as the twelve girls high-kicked their way on stage. Harry ran off and returned, pushing a wheelbarrow into which he tipped his unwelcome visitor. The pair left to gales of laughter while the dancers good-naturedly continued their performance.

After the interval there was another short visit by Harry, followed by the dancing troupe. The main act was a pianist whose records were selling well and who, according to Liz's boss, was going to be the next big thing in the world of popular music.

Liz slipped out quietly as the performer took his bow. She was heading towards her chalet when she heard someone call her name.

'Did you enjoy the show?' Rob Douglas was walking towards her.

'I did, thanks. My first visit to the theatre at Rainbows.'

'A little bird tells me you're going into blue and white.'

Liz gasped. 'I didn't think anyone knew yet.'

He laughed. 'Actually, your boss told me.'

'Did he indeed? Well, I don't think for one moment you can include me on the schedule. Stuart Boyd's not going to want me skimping on office work, now is he?'

'No, but it's going to be useful having someone both decorative and intelligent available.'

'There are plenty of people on the staff who fit that description.'

'I'm sorry, Liz. I didn't mean to belittle any of my colleagues, and now I've gone and upset you, when all I wanted to do was ask if you'd like to come out with me tomorrow.'

She frowned. 'But surely that's not allowed.'

'Not if we're both in uniform it isn't, but I have the day off. I'm tied up in the morning but if you skip your evening meal, we could meet up? He hesitated. 'Maybe have a bite to eat outside the camp?'

Liz remained silent, her thoughts in turmoil. Although she'd only just met Rob, she liked him very much; but the last thing she wanted was for him to think she was an easy conquest. Anyway, he must have an inflated opinion of himself.

'It's nice of you, Rob, but I have rather a lot to do tomorrow.'

'I know how demanding your job is, but surely you're not planning on spending all evening in the office?'

She'd backed herself into a difficult

position now. She didn't want to tell lies, but nor did she want to admit she too was due a day off. After all, it was her first one in her new job, and she was looking forward to exploring the town and walking along the beach at last. And as she'd packed up and left home in such a hurry, she should also see if the hairdresser on site could shampoo and trim her hair.

Luckily she was saved by a group of holidaymakers leaving the coffee bar and spotting Rob beneath the lights of the walkway. They surged towards him, joshing and asking if he was on his way to the Buckingham Ballroom.

'I bagsie the last waltz with you,' said a cheeky grandma.

Liz chuckled. This was her Cinderella moment, except she had no glass coach waiting, nor even a passing pumpkin to hop into. Duty called the Rainbow chief, as he very well knew, but that didn't stop him giving her one last beseeching glance as he was swept away.

One of the men turned back and called, 'Aren't you coming too, lass?'

Liz smiled and called, 'Thanks for thinking of me, but not this time.'

Sounds of music and laughter floated across the concourse from the ballroom as she watched the group enter the building. Rob turned back one more time before disappearing through the doorway.

Maybe she shouldn't have stood there watching, but Liz returned his wave. Of course she liked Rob; liked him very much. But it was far too early in the season to risk beginning a relationship with one of her fellow workers — especially the man who attracted attention from countless campers, even if their crushes faded faster than their holiday suntans when they left at the week's end.

★   ★   ★

Next morning's wake-up call startled Liz as usual, until she remembered this was her day off and if she wanted to stay in bed, she could. She raised her head to check if Jenny was still asleep, but the counterpane was pushed back and her chalet mate was nowhere to be seen. A few minutes later, while Liz debated the lure of a lie-in against going for breakfast, Jenny returned from the bathroom.

'Liz, could I possibly swap breakfast sittings with you just for today? I would've asked you last night, but it didn't occur to me when you said you had the day off.'

Liz raised herself on one elbow. 'Will anyone mind?'

'I doubt it. As long as you and I don't mind sitting with a table full of people we don't know! And that's part of the job, isn't it? It happens every changeover day.'

Liz snuggled back beneath the covers. 'Are you going into the office? I can't believe that boss of mine's that much of a slave driver.'

Her eyes widened as she saw Jenny

selecting a pair of dark green linen slacks and a blouse the colour of primroses. 'Do you have a day off too, Jenny?' She decided not to mention Rob also being freed from duties.

'I have some urgent business to attend to so I need to catch the London train.'

For a moment, Liz wondered if Jenny and Rob were off to the city together. But if that were so, why would he not make the most of those precious hours and escort Jenny back on an evening train?

Jenny slipped her feet into strappy sandals while pre-empting Liz's next question. 'Don't worry about the office. Angie will type the schedule to help Colin, and you must have your rest day, Liz. Looks as if the weather's holding.' She picked up her cream leather shoulder bag. 'And I'd better get going.'

'Yes, don't miss your train. If you're back in time, I'll probably be in the coffee bar around eight o'clock.'

But Jenny was already halfway through the door. 'Bye,' she called.

So Jenny knew Rob wasn't on duty that day. Liz couldn't believe the sharp pang of jealousy she'd suffered at the thought of her two new friends going out together, and scolded herself for being silly. What she should focus upon was the prospect of spending a whole day alone. After the last busy days, with people in and out of the office and the camp brimming with holidaymakers and so full of life, it would feel strange wandering wherever she wished and being at liberty to sit down at a café table and read her book without clock watching. Would she feel a sense of bliss, or would she feel bereft? She'd soon find out.

★　★　★

It was four o'clock in the afternoon before Liz made her way along the promenade. Her feet sank into soft sand as she left the stone slope leading down to the beach. Plenty of sun worshipers were still around, probably including several groups of holidaymakers from Rainbows. Although the swimming facilities were great on site, the chance to take a dip in the briny was always a big draw, especially if families had children who'd brought buckets and spades with them.

Liz walked across the soft golden sand and onto the firmer surface of the area recently covered by seawater. The breeze ruffled her newly trimmed hair and she lifted her face to the sun, hoping her nose wouldn't turn as red as the camp clown's by morning. In the distance the ocean sparkled beneath a clear blue sky. It was the perfect British picture-postcard beach scene in a June promising more good weather to come.

'Fancy meeting you here.'

She whirled round and came face to face with Rob.

'Don't worry, Liz, I wasn't following you. I just happened to look up and see who was walking ahead of me.'

She swallowed. 'Sorry, Rob, I was miles away.'

'Mind if I keep you company? Please say if you'd rather be on your own.'

He sounded diffident, much more so than he had yesterday. But surely he couldn't be shy? He was the most popular male Rainbow host, as well as their chief. She must be mistaken. But he was looking anxiously at her, his blue eyes serious, his ready smile no longer to the forefront.

'No, it's all right. Please stay,' she said.

They began walking again. Rob pushed his hands into his trouser pockets, and again she noticed how he adjusted his stride to suit her shorter one.

'Yesterday evening, when we were talking, it didn't work out at all as I hoped,' he said. 'I'm sorry about that.'

'It's the price for being so popular.'

'It's the uniform and name badge, I'm afraid.'

'You're like a magnet.'

'It's the same with the other Rainbows,' he said, sounding defensive.

'Don't be modest. Yes, the others are sought after, but it's like you're one of the Beatles — or Cliff Richard maybe.'

'No way — I can't sing for toffee!'

'So you're not looking to become a star?'

'Nope. I like the organisational side. That's what I've set my sights on.'

'You're after Stuart Boyd's job?'

He chuckled. 'He's an excellent manager. Yes, I'd like to go into management one day, but I still have loads to learn. Stuart's very supportive of me.'

'I'm enjoying working for him, even though some days can be very hectic.'

'Manic at times, but I think you're coping well.'

'Thanks, but we shouldn't be talking about work when it's still our day off.'

'Liz . . . ' He hesitated.

'Yes, Rob?'

'Oh heck, why can't I put on the charm like I do with the glamorous grandmothers and the teeny boppers hanging round the swimming pool?'

'I'm glad you don't. With me, I mean. I like you just the way you are.'

He sucked in his breath. 'Does that mean . . . ? What I'm trying to say is, would you come out for a meal with me this evening?'

What had happened to her firm resolution not to begin the kind of friendship that could so easily turn into something deeper? Liz couldn't say, but she knew she wanted to spend more time with Rob and get to know him better, now he'd proved he wasn't the shallow flirt she'd suspected him of being.

'I'd like that very much, but only as long as we go Dutch.'

'Oh, no! I asked you out, Miss Lane. I insist it's my treat.'

She stopped walking. He followed suit and turned to face her.

'I suppose it'd be churlish to argue.'

He smiled. 'It would indeed. So that's a yes?'

'It is. Thank you for the invitation.'

'Super duper. To me, you look lovely

in that outfit, but if you want to go back to your chalet I'll understand. I do have two older sisters, you know.'

She pretended to concentrate hard. 'Well, if your sisters would get changed, that's good enough for me.'

He stopped, picked up a pretty shell and pressed it into her hand.

'What's that for?'

'How about a keepsake of our first walk together on the beach?'

Oh no — he was a romantic, and here she was loving it. Time for distraction tactics. 'Now then, as for what I should wear . . . Well, um, it depends where you're taking me.' She pushed the shell inside her pocket.

'How long since you ate?'

'I found a little café and had cheese on toast for lunch. That was at half past twelve.'

'In that case, I'd like to take you to a hotel about five miles from here.'

She felt as though an icy hand had gripped her heart. What kind of girl did he think she was?

'Liz?'

'Why would you want to take me to a hotel?' She'd tried to sound suitably stern.

Rob chuckled. 'I'm doing it again, aren't I? Getting things all wrong. I know the couple that run the hotel because they're friends of the boss and his wife. Rest assured, if I had any funny tricks in mind, I wouldn't be taking you somewhere knowing that Stuart and Angie would be sure to find out within twenty-four hours.' He swiped his forefinger across his throat and rolled his eyes.

Liz had to laugh at him. He looked so contrite. 'You can't blame me for thinking the worst, Rob. A few of the Rainbows have a bit of a reputation, if you don't mind me saying so.'

He nodded. 'That's as may be. But I hope I'm not included in that group.'

'No,' she said softly. 'To be fair, I've heard nothing but good things about you, Rob.'

He took one of her hands in his. 'Let's walk back. On the way you can decide whether you want to get changed or not. And I meant to tell you I like your new hairdo.'

'Thank you. But this hotel you mentioned, is it posh? Do the guests change for dinner?'

'I've only been there twice, but each time everyone in the dining room looked smart. Now it occurs to me it's definitely a place where I should wear a suit. Is that all right? The food's great and there's a little terrace where we can sit and enjoy a drink before we eat.'

'It sounds lovely and yes, I'd like to freshen up and change into a dress.'

'Fair enough. Now, I'll take you into the camp via the service entrance at the back. That way, we can each get into our chalet without meeting too many happy holidaymakers and having to stop and make light conversation.'

* * *

'This is even more tranquil than I imagined.' Liz picked up her glass and sipped the cool drink.

'The view from where I'm sitting is fantastic.'

Liz felt herself blush. The admiration in Rob's eyes was unmistakeable, and the warm feeling it gave her was wonderful. What girl wouldn't enjoy being wined and dined by a good-looking young man?

'Seriously, Rob, all those trees in the background and the lush plants and flowers — it's as if we're somewhere abroad, don't you think?'

'I know what you mean. The hotel nestled in a little valley means this garden's a suntrap.'

Liz patted each of her cheeks in turn and touched her nose.

'You've caught the sun beautifully. Don't worry, no red nose, only a few cute freckles.'

'That's a relief.'

'I can't decide whether that's your perfume smelling of roses or whether it's the roses on the bush behind you. Both, maybe?'

'I wouldn't dare comment, but

thanks so much for bringing me here, Rob. I never even knew you had a car.'

'I cannot tell a lie; it belongs to my father. He and my mum are spending a month in Scotland with my eldest sister and her family. Maggie's just had her first baby.'

'How lovely! So you're an uncle?'

'You bet. And in exchange for driving my folks to Euston Station this morning and collecting them on their return, I'm allowed use of the Vauxhall.'

It didn't sound as though he'd been in London with Jenny. Relief flooded through Liz. Whatever was the matter with her? It was as if one half of her was fighting the other.

'I've been saving up for driving lessons,' she said, gathering her wits.

'I could teach you, if you like.'

She laughed. 'Goodness, that's a very kind offer, but I doubt I could learn in just a few hours.' The thought of Rob sitting beside her, helping her work out what her hands and feet were supposed to be doing, gave her a light-headed feeling, unless such a sensation could be caused by the drink sparkling in the champagne glass before her. She held it by its stem and twirled it slowly round on the wrought-iron tabletop.

'I could teach you the basic things,' he said. 'These light evenings, we could cover a lot in an hour.'

'Your breaks in the schedule are meant as just that,' she said.

'Yes, miss.'

'I'm serious, Rob. You work very hard, you put in long hours, and you don't need to be giving me driving lessons on top of all your other duties. Mr Boyd would be horrified.'

'It's none of his business as long as I do my job properly. We might even get the same day off again next week.'

'I think it's going to be Tuesdays for me from now on.'

'We'll manage.'

'I hardly know you. I'm not sure what to say.'

'Then say yes. It would be my pleasure; and as for getting to know each other, what better way than a driving lesson?'

'Hmm, well . . . maybe it'd be sensible to find out whether I actually like sitting behind the steering wheel before I fork out money to a driving school.'

'That's my girl.' He caught the attention of the waiter. 'I'll just see if they have any Blue Nun on ice.'

'Wine as well?' She felt a frisson of alarm. He couldn't be earning a great deal of money, but she wouldn't dream of embarrassing him, especially as their surroundings were so luxurious.

He turned back to her. 'I've ordered a half bottle. Don't panic. I have no intention of getting you or myself drunk.'

She pretended to shudder. 'I can't imagine the awfulness of trying to decipher your handwriting tomorrow afternoon if I was fighting a hangover!'

'Cheeky!' But he was smiling. 'Now, have you made up your mind what you want to eat? I don't know about you, but given half a chance, I could eat this table.'

4

It's Too Soon to Know

For once, Liz awoke before the bedroom-ceiling speaker crackled into life. She lay quietly, thinking about the events of the previous day, particularly the time spent with Rob.

He was ambitious, without a doubt. But he tended to underestimate his abilities, and that intrigued her. Maybe his father had been very stern and praise hadn't come Rob's way too often. She smiled as the notes of the now very familiar wake-up song spilled from the speaker. Time to push back the covers.

'Goodness!' She couldn't help speaking aloud.

The bed opposite was empty. Last night Liz had gone to sleep wondering when Jenny would return from her long day out, but to find her still not back was, to say the least, puzzling. Her chalet mate's bag of toiletries stood on the chest beside her bed and her robe lay across the counterpane, so she couldn't be already in the bathroom.

Surely Jenny hadn't spent the night with a boyfriend? Was that the reason she hadn't been more forthcoming as to how she was spending her day off? She lived somewhere in the London area, so it would be logical if she had a boy-friend back home. But if he was someone special, why did she choose to work away from him at Rainbows? Had he persuaded her to spend the night with him? Surely Jenny wasn't the kind of girl who'd do such a thing. The stop-over must have been unplanned, or else Jenny would surely have taken an over-night bag.

Liz's thoughts remained in turmoil as she washed and dressed for the first time in her white accordion-pleated skirt, cornflower-blue blouse and blazer. She pushed her feet into white shoes with

Cuban heels and slipped a clean handkerchief in one pocket and her purse in the other. She squinted at her reflection in the solitary mirror the two girls shared and thought how strange it seemed to be wearing the well-known uniform.

Outside, other staff members were locking their chalet doors behind them. One or two called a greeting and said it was good to see her wearing uniform.

A piercing wolf-whistle stopped her in her tracks just outside the dining room. 'Well, if it's not my glamour girl! You wait till the camp photographer sees you in that uniform. He'll have your picture on a publicity poster before you know it!'

'Harry,' said Liz, trying to look stern. 'I might have known it was you shattering the morning peace.'

He made a mock bow. 'Just making my feelings known, darling heartbreaker. You look lovely, but then, you'd look like a Hollywood star wearing a sack tied round the middle with string.'

Liz couldn't help but laugh. He was

such a charmer, but she knew it was all part of his act. 'What rubbish you talk, Harry.'

He pretended to dab tears away. 'I might've known you didn't take me seriously. Could it be you've given your heart to some other lovelorn swain?'

She stared back at him. Surely he didn't know she'd been out with Rob the evening before? Were there no secrets in this place?

'I'm here to earn my living,' she said. 'Not to find a husband.'

'Of course, me darling.' Harry winked at her. 'I must go; but if ever you need a shoulder to cry on, don't forget Uncle Harry.'

He held the swing door open for her, and she was tempted to ask him what on earth he meant but thought better of it. If he really did know about her night out with Rob, was he warning her of possible heartbreak ahead? Should she have stuck to her original perception regarding the charming chief host?

Liz took her seat at the head of her

table and purposely didn't glance across to see if Rob Douglas was in his. She exchanged morning greetings with a couple of families already seated and sipped a glass of orange juice while she waited for her tea and toast to arrive.

Her thoughts returned to Jenny, though she tried her best to hold a conversation with the woman seated to her right. But her concern over her chalet mate's non-appearance made it difficult to discuss what the woman's teenage daughter should wear when entering the Rainbow Princess beauty contest taking place that afternoon.

When she finished her breakfast, Liz walked to the entertainments building and began to look at matters needing immediate attention, but she found it difficult to concentrate. Her boss soon buzzed her to come through to his office, though she knew exactly what she was going to say. Staff members were entitled to stay out of the holiday camp before beginning work each day, but anxiety was tearing at her. Whatever

Jenny got up to in her personal life, Liz would never forgive herself if something had happened to her friend and she hadn't reported her absence.

'Come in.' Mr Boyd looked up from the sheet of paper on the desk before him. Liz recognised it as the daily schedule someone, probably Angie, had typed the day before. 'Sit down, Liz. Did you enjoy your day off?'

'Very much, thanks.' She bit her lip. 'The thing is, Mr Boyd, something's bothering me, and I really think I should take advice. If Angie was on duty this morning, I'd slip in and talk to her, but — '

'My wife's not working today. Is this, um, something personal? I'll give you our home phone number if you'd like to speak to her.'

Liz felt her cheeks warming. 'No, it's nothing to do with my personal life. It's to do with Jenny.'

He banged his forehead with his fist. 'Oh dear, I clean forgot to mention it, Liz. I must apologise, because when

Jenny rang me, she specifically asked if I'd give you a message.'

Relief flooded through Liz. 'I'll forgive you as long as she's all right, Mr Boyd.'

'Just be glad I'm not your secretary. I think you'd have given me the sack by now if that were the case.'

Liz smiled politely and waited for him to get to the point.

'Jenny asked me to let you know she won't be back for a few more days. Without disclosing anything confidential, I can tell you she's officially on compassionate leave.'

'Oh my goodness, poor Jenny. And there was I thinking . . . Well, it doesn't matter what I was thinking.'

'I don't think she knew yesterday that she'd be staying away. Our telephone conversation this morning was brief, but I must confess I'd temporarily forgotten you two were chalet mates.'

'We haven't had time to become close friends, as most of the time we're together we're fast asleep.'

Mr Boyd cleared his throat. 'Indeed. Well, Jenny's absence means we have to look at the daily schedule and make a few adjustments.'

'Of course. I've noticed that Rob usually puts her down to work with the children, so I imagine she'll be missed.'

'Yes, she started off working in the crèche, but we transferred her to the entertainments side last summer. She got on so well, we asked her to return this year.'

'I imagine you have someone else suitable among the Rainbows? I can go and tell whoever it is you choose.'

'You don't need to do that.' He sat back in his chair and tapped a pen against his front teeth.

'I know my way around the site now, so I'll be back in time to take dictation before you meet with the publicity manager.'

'Liz.' Mr Boyd leaned forward and smiled gently. 'I can't think of anyone better than you to stand in for Jenny today. I've already discussed the situation with Rob Douglas, and he agrees you're perfect for the job.'

'Me?'

'Your face is a picture.' Mr Boyd leaned back in his chair. 'Everyone says you're friendly and easy to get on with. Rob tells me you've talked to him about your kid brother and some of the places you've taken him and the games you've played. All we want is the right kind of person to give the team a hand, and no one expects you to do anything other than help the children enjoy the holiday. Happy youngsters means happy mums and dads, not to mention grandparents.'

'But do you want me to start now? What will happen about your letters?' She felt a prickle of anxiety. Would she be up to this new role?

'They'll keep until tomorrow if necessary, and it won't hurt me to make a few phone calls myself. Now, it would be great if you could find Colin and report to him. What a good job I decided you should begin wearing blue and white.'

Liz stood at the side of the children's playground, keeping an eye on the rowdiest of the little boys. A small girl with her hair in plaits tugged at her sleeve.

'What is it, love?'

'I can't find Aunty Jenny. She wasn't here yesterday either, and I miss her.' The child's bottom lip quivered.

Liz crouched so she could address the little girl eye to eye. The child wore a name badge safety-pinned to her pink cotton frock. 'Hello, Susan. I expect Aunty Jenny's missing you too. She'd really rather be here with all of you than away in dusty old London.'

The child's face brightened. 'Shall I wait by the first-aid hut in case she comes back? That's where we're supposed to go if we get lost.'

'Do you know, I think as soon as she returns, Aunty Jenny will be looking out for you. But she wouldn't want you to miss out on having fun while she's away. What kind of things do you like doing?'

'I like the skipping games and playing statues. I'm good at keeping very still.'

Liz stood up and held out her hand. 'Come on then, let's see if Uncle Colin will let us play statues next.'

The little girl trotted alongside Liz. 'You're nice, too. Will you be here until Aunty Jenny comes back?'

Liz prayed for guidance. 'Um, I'm not sure yet; but I promise that if I have to work in my office tomorrow, I'll come and see how you're getting on when I'm on my break.'

Susan began to skip as, hand in hand, she and Liz walked across to where Colin was making sure turns on the seesaw were achieved by fair means.

'Uncle Colin, this young lady with the lovely pink frock would really like to play a game of statues. Is that all right?'

He grinned. 'You're in charge, Aunty Liz.'

She fixed him with a look. But the morning flew by, and Liz had gained a new fan. When Susan's parents arrived to collect her precisely at noon, their daughter sped towards them and flung herself at her mum.

'Can I come back tomorrow again? It was fun.'

Her mum smiled at Liz. 'Thank you so much. Sue was a bit worried when Jenny wasn't here again, but thanks to you she seems to have settled. It's so nice to know she's well cared for and playing with other children while we enjoy our morning game of tennis.'

'That's what we're here for,' said Liz. She couldn't believe she'd said that. When Stuart Boyd told her what he had in mind, she'd been very unsure. Now, watching Susan skip along, holding on to a parent on each side, she realised she relished the change.

'We close until two o'clock, but then you already know that, don't you?' Colin gave her a friendly hug around the shoulders. 'Bet you didn't think you'd be refereeing a crowd of children when you sent off your CV to head office.'

'No, indeed I didn't, but it's good to see what kinds of things you all do. You know I'm based in the entertainments centre, except when I flit about the camp, delivering messages and instructions.'

'Well, after lunch we have a treasure hunt, and I haven't written all the clues yet. Could you spare me ten minutes? I'm trying not to use the same old ones, and two heads should be better than one, especially if one of them is mine.'

'I'm not sure I'll be any good, but I'll give it a go.'

'We'll need to get a move on. You're on first sitting, aren't you?'

'Yes.' She looked up at the sky. 'It's getting a bit overcast. I hope it doesn't rain.'

'If it does, we'll take them all into the ballroom and play silly games, then sit them down and Aunty Liz can tell them a story.'

'Hey, wait a minute! I'm hopeless at . . . ' Her voice tailed off. Colin was hurrying towards the nearest seat and she had no option but to follow. Trunks, she thought. The jungle mural near the swimming pool included baby elephants.

'I've thought of a clue,' she said, sitting down beside Colin.

★   ★   ★

'I have a bone to pick with you,' Liz said as she caught up with Rob on her way back to the children's playground.

'Oh dear. I wondered when we'd bump into each other.'

She tried to keep a calm expression, but she was hit for six when he turned to her and she saw the tenderness in his eyes. This wasn't at all what should be happening. Not to sensible Elizabeth Lane it shouldn't.

'Well,' she went on, 'I'm not sure whether to be cross with you, or pleased you suggested I stand in for Jenny.'

'That sounds ominous. So how did this morning go? I've been thinking about you.'

Fortunately, sensible Elizabeth beat

flibbertigibbet Liz into submission, so she didn't blurt out how she'd been thinking of him too. 'I've had a good morning, thanks, Rob. I wouldn't want to do this for a whole season though.'

'Ah, so you miss bossing old Stuart around, do you?'

Liz laughed. 'You may be chief Rainbow, but that doesn't stop me from fixing you with one of my hard stares.'

He sighed. 'I knew it! You're bossing me around now.'

'Chance would be a fine thing.' She was determined to keep things on a light-hearted level.

'I enjoyed last night.'

Her heart had decided to play skipping games all on its own. 'Well, I had a lovely time too.'

'Did you think any more about those driving lessons?'

'I haven't really had much of a chance. What with finding out Jenny has to be away for a while and trying not to cause too much havoc for Colin, it honestly hasn't entered my mind.'

'Well, do give it some thought when you can. You know I'm happy to help, and besides, I enjoy your company.'

'Yes. It's just that I — '

'Look, Liz — if you're not interested, you only have to say the word and I'll back off.'

Was that what she wanted? It would make life easier in some ways. But Rob Douglas was getting under her skin, and the trouble was, she couldn't bear the thought of him giving her the cold shoulder.

'I didn't mean to sound ungrateful. Maybe when Jenny's back and things are normal again, work-wise, we could meet up. Only if you think you can put up with me, though. And it goes without saying, I insist on paying for the petrol.'

He looked at her and this time she met his gaze. 'If I can put up with you! Liz, you have absolutely no fears where that's concerned.'

He moved a step closer. She felt as if someone had turned up the thermostat on the afternoon's humid atmosphere, bringing it to sizzling point as they stood looking into one another's eyes. She must move. People would notice; wonder what was going on. Rob looked as though he wanted to say something else to her. Something important. She mustn't let that happen, not with such a lot of the summer season still stretching ahead of them.

She looked away and spotted Colin. 'Ah, there's my new boss,' she called. To her relief, he came jogging across the concourse towards them.

'Wotcha,' he said. 'Come on then, Aunty. It's time to brave the little monsters again. Slightly different lot this afternoon, of course.'

'Little monsters indeed!' Liz rolled her eyes at Rob. 'He's brilliant with them, isn't he?'

'He is,' Rob answered, 'and you make a terrific team, you two. Have a good afternoon.' And then he was gone.

'Methinks our chief is smitten, Miss Lane.'

'Don't be daft, Col. Rob can't help but charm everyone he meets.'

'If you say so.'

They walked on together. Liz's heart righted itself and settled back to its normal rhythm. It was time to go back to work. But if Rob did have feelings for her, and people were beginning to notice, she'd have to tread very carefully indeed.

5

I Remember You

That evening after supper, Liz wandered towards the ballroom. Although she wore uniform, because of her main role as Stuart Boyd's secretary, she wasn't expected to join in the goodnight routines after the orchestra played the last waltz. She'd been relieved to hear it after receiving her blue-and-white kit, because she'd have found the commitment difficult, given she normally arrived at the office by eight-thirty each morning. Yet as her boss had advised her, she was welcome to join in the dancing on the condition that she didn't partner any of the male Rainbows, or even spend too long in conversation with another host or hostess.

Liz was still much too shy to

approach one of the holidaymakers and ask him to dance. So she didn't know whether to feel relieved or apprehensive when, as the orchestra began playing 'I Remember You', a tall man with dark brown hair approached her and held out his hand.

'May I beg a dance?'

Liz saw his gaze take in her name badge. At once his expression changed.

'I can't believe it. So it really is you!'

'I'm sorry, have we met somewhere before?' She could have bitten her tongue off. Every girl knew to beware of the old chat-up line, and here she was the one spouting it.

The stranger took her arm. Except he seemed to know her, didn't he? But for the life of her she couldn't place him.

He steered her towards a table. 'I thought you looked familiar, but it's been a long time. May I fetch you a drink, Liz?'

'No, thanks. I'm happy to dance with you — but first, I think you should explain why you think you know me.'

He sighed. 'You are Liz Lane, aren't you? If not, I owe you an apology.'

'That is my name, yes.'

'I know I shouldn't expect you to remember me. I must be eight or nine years older than you are. You were friends with my little sister at school, but I wasn't around much.'

'Are you telling me you're Pam's brother?' She had a vague recollection of a young man in jeans. Not only had he been far too grown-up to bother with two thirteen year-olds, but he'd left home to join the army, and Liz hadn't given a thought to him since.

'Yes, I'm Mike Parks. Phew, for a minute there I thought I must've changed beyond recognition.'

'Sorry, Mike — you took me by surprise but of course I remember you now.'

'And I remember you, Liz. I remember you very well.'

She was about to ask him how his sister was getting on when he shook his head, his expression bemused. 'I can't believe I've bumped into you after all this time. Why don't we have a dance? Maybe you can help me with a certain problem I'm hoping to solve.'

Liz felt a tremor ripple down her spine. Mike sounded far too intense for her liking, but she nodded and followed him onto the dance floor. While the band played a lively quickstep, she somehow managed to follow her partner without stepping on his toes. He seemed in no hurry to continue their conversation, and when the next dance proved to be a catchy cha-cha, she concentrated on the rhythm and Mike did the same.

'One more?'

'Yes, if you like.' Liz was enjoying the dancing and in no hurry to be interrogated over something that could only involve the past. If he hoped to find clues to some dark secret, he'd be out of luck.

But this time they were dancing a waltz, and she realised its soft and gentle rhythm would make it much easier for Mike to question her. He'd seemed so surprised to see her that her original concern that he must have contacted her parents and discovered her whereabouts couldn't be the case. Her family still lived in the same house, although Mike and Pam's folks had moved to another town soon after the two girls had left school.

'Are you still in the army? And how's Pam these days? Is she still nursing?' Liz knew she was gabbling but somehow couldn't stop. 'I'm afraid we're only in touch via Christmas cards,' she said. 'What a coincidence that you should turn up here and notice me.'

'It is indeed. Yes, Pam's still nursing, engaged to be married, and she's very well, as far as I'm aware. Next time we talk on the phone, I'll tell her she should drop you a line.' He hesitated. 'Look, Liz, to come straight to the point, after I decided I didn't want to sign on again for a military career, I applied to train as a teacher. While I was waiting to start college in the autumn, I got a job as a holiday rep and was sent to work in Mallorca.'

'That must have been fun. One day I'd like to book a package holiday and see the island for myself.'

'It's beautiful. I hope to go back one day, just for a holiday of course.'

Liz saw the faraway look in his eyes just before she noticed the bandleader eying her. Then Colin danced past, partnering a grey-haired woman who had a corkscrew perm and who was chatting nonstop. Colin mouthed something at Liz as her gaze met his; something that she realised meant she should move on.

Of course! She hadn't danced with a different partner since Mike had asked her to take the floor. Colin was right to remind her, because hosts and hostesses were supposed to mingle with the campers, not dance every dance with only one of them. At that moment she was convinced all the Rainbows in the ballroom must be wondering what she was playing at. How stupid was that? Her reputation was at stake here.

She took a deep breath. 'Mike, I'm not officially on duty in the ballroom but we do have a kind of protocol, so I should really encourage you to ask someone else to dance. Please don't think this is anything personal; it's because I'm in uniform.'

She felt his fingers tighten around hers. 'I'm aware of the drill, Liz, but I'm finding it hard to get around to explaining why I booked in here.'

'I don't understand. Why would this involve me?' Surely whatever his questions were, they could have nothing to do with her old school friend and their lives a decade earlier? Liz was puzzled as to why he hadn't got straight to the point.

'Believe me, I'd no idea you were working here. This is about a girl called Jenny.'

Liz stopped dancing at once and stared back at him as if he'd suddenly grown two heads.

'Does Jenny Carter still work here, Liz? If so, I imagine you must know her.'

Luckily the music ended in a crescendo of soaring trumpet notes and the happy dancers applauded and whistled their approval, some drifting off the beautifully sprung dance floor, some couples waiting for the next set to begin.

'Shall we have that drink now?' Mike took both her hands in his as the bandleader announced the names of the songs he wanted everyone to jive to. 'How about getting out of here and going to the coffee bar? I don't want to get you into trouble, but you said you weren't on duty, and if you can help me find Jenny I'll be halfway towards making a dream come true.'

Liz's uneasy feeling wasn't going to disappear in a hurry. He was firing questions at her, and how on earth did she know what to say to the man? It sounded as though he'd come to Rainbows on a mission. But what if Jenny didn't welcome Mike's attentions? Was he an ex-boyfriend? Maybe she didn't want anything else to do with him. And while Jenny was on compassionate leave, she didn't need anything else to add to her problems.

While Liz searched for the right words, words that wouldn't either hurt or anger Mike Parks, help arrived in the form of someone very pretty who wore her yellow-and-white uniform as though it was a Norman Hartnell creation.

'Now, now, Liz,' said Cathy.

Liz thanked her lucky stars. The leader of the dance troupe was doing an excellent impression of a stern teacher but couldn't stop her lips from twitching.

'We can't let you monopolise this nice young man.' Cathy beamed at Mike. 'I'm sure Liz will spare you for one dance. To be honest, I've spent so much time on my feet today, including performing, they're screaming for mercy tonight; and I'd like a partner who won't step on my toes. You look as though you know what you're doing.'

To Liz's relief, Mike laughed. 'I'm flattered,' he said. 'I recognise you from last night's show, so it's great to meet you. I enjoyed your performance very much. Sorry if I'm monopolising Liz, but she and I used to be near neighbours, and I'm hoping she'll allow me to buy her a coffee.'

'Oh, but you should stay and enjoy yourself, Mike,' said Liz, words tumbling out in relief. 'Quite honestly, tomorrow would be better for me. I really have had a busy day, and you'll get more sense out of me in the morning. If you come to the coffee bar in the entertainments centre, around eleven, I'll take my break then.'

'All settled,' said Cathy, grabbing Mike's hand. 'Come on then, Mr Twinkle Toes. Let's show 'em how it's done!'

Liz fled, leaving the other two to head for the dance floor. Mike seemed happy to be kidnapped, and it hadn't escaped her notice that Cathy was wearing that captivating scent of hers again. Mike was probably bowled over; and the dancer, bless her heart, had provided a much-needed breathing space. Maybe one of the other Rainbows would know whether Jenny would welcome seeing Mike or not. Colin might be the one to try first, as the two usually worked together, and Liz knew he'd known Jenny since she first started working for Rainbows. But on reflection, it might be best to consult with Angie. Liz was in a delicate position, especially having been friendly with Mike's sister at a stage when they practically lived in one another's houses during the summer holidays. She could hardly refuse to speak to Mike, especially as she hadn't denied Jenny was working at the camp. But Liz feared revealing information about a colleague who was obviously going through a difficult time, and who might well not return to work for a while yet.

She decided not to stop off for a comforting hot drink after all. If Mike should turn up, she'd find it difficult

not to let him sit down with her and she
didn't think she could face an inquisi-
tion. She hurried back through the soft
June evening, calling goodnights to
holidaymakers heading for their own
chalets. What a difference her blue-and-
white uniform made to her popularity
rating!

★　★　★

Liz regained consciousness as the
eighth line of the morning wake-up
song penetrated her brain. 'I doubt very
much that everything's going my way,'
she muttered, swinging her legs from
the narrow bed.

The song was far too optimistic for
her current mood. Why hadn't she been
more assertive with Mike? She should
have told him all she knew was that
Jenny was unable to work at the
moment, and he'd better make an
appointment with the entertainments
manager or with personnel if he wanted
to contact her.

Wasn't that a little mean, though? As she walked towards the dining hall, she decided she could at least offer to deliver a letter to Jenny on her return. With any luck, Mike would have left the camp by then, and it would be up to Jenny as to whether she wrote to him or not.

'You look as if you've lost half a crown and found sixpence.'

Startled, she glanced across to where Rob stood, hands in pockets, smiling at her. He had such a lovely lopsided grin, it was no wonder he attracted such an adoring fan club.

'Sorry,' she said. 'I was miles away.'

'I hope all those miles didn't take you to the depths of misery. Please don't tell me that.' His face suddenly revealed more than she'd bargained for.

Liz found a smile. 'It's a bit tricky. You know when you feel as if you're piggy in the middle?'

He nodded. 'Poor you. Is this something I can help with?'

'Thanks, Rob, but I think it's best if I ask Angie for some advice.'

'No one better.' He glanced at his watch. 'Come on, let's walk the rest of the way together. I wanted to tell you I've changed my day off so it's the same as yours.' He glanced sideways at her. 'Well, that went down like a lead balloon!'

'No, no, I didn't mean to be rude. I was just feeling a bit overwhelmed by everything, that's all.'

'I made it clear to Stuart that I'd offered to give you driving lessons, and — I quote — he said, 'I think that's an admirable plan.' So there!'

'Goodness, Rob, you sounded just like that boss of ours. Why on earth doesn't he put you up on stage, doing impersonations like Mike Yarwood?'

Rob shuddered. 'No thanks; I'd die a thousand deaths. Anyway, you tell me what time you'd like us to get going on Tuesday, and I'll make sure the car's clean and fuelled up ready to go. My time's my own, for once.'

Liz decided not to worry whether he was hinting at spending a little more of that time with her, rather than only an hour or two's instruction. 'How about eleven o'clock?'

'That's fine. Can you remember your way round to the service entrance?'

'Yes, I turn left after the chapel and follow the tarmac road.'

'As opposed to the yellow brick road!' He stopped suddenly. 'Sorry, Liz, I must catch Colin before he's eaten alive by his eager swimming team. See you soon!'

'Yes, I expect so.' She was left gazing after Rob as he sprinted across the wide area in front of their dining hall. The inter-house swimming gala each Friday afternoon was popular with holidaymakers, and Colin was kept busy supervising and offering help to would-be Olympic athletes, as he always told his water babies they should aspire to be.

She hurried to take her seat at the breakfast table. Her gang this week consisted of two families who were friends back in Newcastle and whose three generations had come on holiday together.

They changed places every mealtime, so Liz was getting to know them all, one by one. Today she had one of the young mums on her left and a teenage boy called Ralph on her right. Liz, accustomed to her brother's monosyllabic comments, knew she could converse in grunts if necessary. She took the safer option, said a quick good-morning to everyone, and joined in a conversation about the feast of drama that was showing in the theatre that evening.

* * *

'Angie, do you have time for a quick word?' Liz had jumped up from her chair as the radio presenter passed her office window.

'You just caught me on my break. Could we talk and have some fresh air at the same time? I'll take a coffee back up to my glass cage afterwards.'

Liz glanced at the radio HQ and saw one of the Rainbows, dressed in yellow and white, seated at the console.

'Jean's my usual stand-in,' said Angie. 'We really should get you trained up, Liz.'

'I know, but it's been so hectic!'

'When isn't it?' Angie headed for the staircase. 'Let's go round the side of the building. We're less likely to get nabbed for an autograph.'

Outside, Liz lifted her face to the sun. 'Lovely. Wouldn't it be great to be on holiday?'

Angie chuckled. 'You bet, but this is about something more than holidays, isn't it, Liz?'

The two were strolling along the walkway and Angie pointed to a bench beneath a tree. 'A quick sit-down?'

Liz followed her example. 'I've bumped into someone I used to know when I was much younger,' she said. 'He's staying here this week — and it's pure coincidence, before you ask. His sister used to be my best friend at school.'

'Oh dear, don't tell me he's making a pest of himself?' Angie turned to look at Liz.

'No, not in the least. But he's put me in a difficult position, as he's an old friend of Jenny's and says he's anxious to make contact with her again.'

'I see. And you're not sure how to play this?'

Liz tucked a wayward lock of blonde hair behind one ear. 'What do you think I should say, Angie? I've agreed to see Mike at eleven this morning, just briefly, but I know nothing of Jenny's past history. She might be thrilled to bits to see him again, or — '

'She might run a mile.' Angie bit her lip. 'It does rather put you on the spot, especially as you already know Mike from way back. Why don't you simply stick to what's true? Tell him Jenny's away and suggest he write her a letter, maybe say you'll personally put it into her pigeonhole so she finds it on her return?'

'That's a good idea, Angie. I did wonder whether to suggest that, so you've decided me now. It'll be no good him trying to coax information from me, because I just don't have any.'

Angie glanced at her watch. 'Let's walk back. I'll collect my coffee, and if you return to your desk, that husband of mine can't give you one of his looks if he sees you going downstairs again. On second thought, you can tell him I've asked you to deal with a personal matter on my behalf. He won't dare say a word then!'

Liz hurried back upstairs. Angie was an excellent mentor. It would be great to learn how to operate the Rainbows radio station, but with driving lessons looming and her agony aunt session taking place, Liz needed to concentrate on doing her job as well as she possibly could.

At two minutes to eleven, she stopped typing and tapped on her boss's door. 'Would you like a coffee?' she said. 'I'm just popping downstairs. I promised to run a little errand for Angie.'

'I'm fine, thanks,' said Stuart. 'I thought I saw you with my wife earlier. Any chance of her training you soon?'

Liz laughed. 'She said the same thing. I honestly think I'm going to have to come in on my day off if we want to make this happen.'

'I don't like the sound of that. We work our staff hard, but I won't have my secretary losing precious free time. Let me have a think.'

He picked up his diary and began riffling its pages. Liz took the opportunity to hurry to her rendezvous and caught sight of Mike, who was seated at a table near the bottom of the staircase.

'Liz! He jumped to his feet. 'Thanks for meeting me.'

'Well, I did promise, though I mustn't stay long. Maybe we could join the queue at the counter?'

He guided her, his hand cupping her elbow and making her wonder if he feared she might try to make a getaway. They joined the small line of people waiting to give their orders.

'So,' he said, 'you wouldn't be here unless my assumption was right. You do know Jenny, don't you?'

'As it happens she's my chalet mate.' She watched his face relax. 'But before you get your hopes up, the bad news is that Jenny's on leave at the moment, and I have no idea when she'll be back.'

Mike clicked his tongue with annoyance, but recovered himself quickly to smile at the counter assistant and order their coffees.

'Is there anyone else who'd know?' he said. 'She must have a department head or manager.'

'Her boss is Stuart Boyd, and I'm his secretary. Believe me, the only way to get in touch with Jenny is to write a letter and leave it with us. You have my word she'll receive it when she returns.'

She followed Mike back to the table for two, where they settled themselves.

'At least I know she's actually working here, even though it looks as if I shan't see her.'

'You never know. She might return any time.'

'She's not ill, I hope?'

'Mike, I truly have no idea. All I can

tell you is, she was in good health when she left here. Maybe there's some family emergency and she's caught up in that.'

He nodded, slowly stirring sugar into his cup of coffee. 'I appreciate the help you've given me, Liz.'

She shrugged. 'I've done nothing. If you hadn't bumped into me last night, you'd probably have danced with another of the Rainbows and asked her, wouldn't you?'

'Probably. I've been hoping to bump into Jenny. Stupid of me, I know.' He shook his head. 'I didn't want anyone to wonder about my motives and make a complaint, but what a relief when I spotted you last night. Pam will be pleased to hear about your exciting job when I ring my little sister next.' He glanced at the clock.

Liz sipped her coffee and winced. 'I don't wish to seem rude, but this is so hot, I'd better take my cup upstairs to the office.'

'I understand. But is your boss really

such a slave driver?'

'Not at all, so all the more reason not to take advantage of him!'

Mike shot her a searching look. 'I don't suppose you'd come out for a meal with me this evening, or tomorrow, if that's better for you?'

She didn't want to hurt his feelings, but they had very little in common, from what she could tell. Reminiscences were all very well, but a whole evening trying to make polite conversation didn't appeal. She really couldn't tell him any more about Jenny than she already had.

'I've got quite a lot on this week, Mike. I'm sorry. Maybe we could have a quick coffee on Friday night?'

'I suppose I'll have to make do with that.' He smiled at her. 'I'm playing tennis this afternoon, and I'll probably swim afterwards; maybe catch tonight's theatre performance later. I've palled up with another bloke who's here on his own.'

'Well that sounds like the perfect

holiday schedule to me. Have a great time.' She stood and picked up her cup.

Mike jumped to his feet. 'See you around then, Liz.' He bent to kiss her cheek. 'I'll definitely write that letter.'

6

I Can't Say No

Liz spent the next few days going from her chalet to the dining hall, on to her office, and then to the theatre or to personnel or one of the camp's other departments, delivering messages, checking files, and gaining more and more experience.

To her relief, Mike didn't seek her out again, but he called at her office the afternoon before his departure and she met him later for a coffee as he'd suggested. She ensured the letter he handed over for Jenny was safe in her pigeonhole, awaiting her return.

Liz had soon learnt her boss rarely took a whole day off, even though his wife worked shifts, fitting in with childcare and her colleagues' schedules. She marvelled at the way in which

Angie juggled her various roles. At last, the day before Liz's next day off, Angie asked if she would sit beside her in her 'glass cage', as she called it, to get to know a little about the procedure.

Liz pulled up a chair beside the radio presenter, trying to ignore the butterflies in her stomach. She liked the idea of helping out but dreaded making a fool of herself. How awful if she mixed up her words and the result was heard ringing round the whole of the holiday camp!

'I'll put a medley on after I've made the next announcement,' said Angie. 'You'll have noticed we remind the campers of coming events, to whip up enthusiasm?'

'I have, yes.'

Angie nodded. 'Good. You'll notice that a copy of the daily schedule you type so beautifully sits right beside me here at the console. I'm notified of any last-minute changes by Rob Douglas; or, if he's on a day off, by Colin Skelton.'

Liz nodded.

'Always remember — once you finish speaking, you must flick the switch to close down the microphone.'

'Now that's something I dread forgetting,' said Liz. 'Imagine people hearing me coughing or muttering beneath my breath! What a nightmare.'

'You'll be fine. It'll become second nature, you wait and see.'

'That's what Rob says about driving. I hope I don't drive both of you potty over the next few weeks.'

'Just think how good both these skills are going to look on your CV. Now concentrate on me, not Rob, because I'd like you to make the next announcement and introduce a song after Tommy Steele stops singing the blues.'

Liz's cheeks were warming, and not only because of that crack about Rob. Panic-stricken, she turned to look at Angie. 'You're not serious?'

'Oh but I am. Don't worry, I'll guide you through. What you mustn't do is sit too close to the microphone.' She rattled off a few further bits of advice while Liz listened, trying to appear calmer than she felt.

She looked down at the piece of paper where Angie had typed her play list. The record Liz would announce after Angie handed over to her was a Michael Holliday recording of 'Stairway to Love', so she must remember to do a lead-in to that song.

Angie was already drawing the holiday-makers' attention to the children's Water Babies session and reminding them about the exciting dramatic perfor-mance scheduled to take place in the camp theatre that evening. Then she flicked the switch and got up from her chair. 'Over to you, Liz. Tommy's still singing.'

Liz took the presenter's place and picked up the headphones as soon as she'd settled into Angie's seat. As the song neared its close, she cleared her throat and took a couple of deep breaths. Angie nodded encouragingly.

Liz reached her hand out to flick the

magic switch and her first announcement percolated through the sound system. 'This is your Rainbows Radio stand-in presenter, Liz, speaking to you. Please don't forget the Miss Sweetheart beauty contest that's taking place beside the swimming pool at three o'clock today. If there are any more contestants who haven't yet registered, you still have until one o'clock to do so. Rainbows Geoff and Marion will be delighted to add you to the list.'

With relief, Liz invited holidaymakers to climb the 'Stairway of Love' with velvet-voiced Michael Holliday and, despite her trembling hand, managed to set the needle on the disk spinning on the turntable. As soon as she heard the jaunty opening chords through her headphones, she switched off the microphone and sat back in the chair.

'Well done,' said a voice from the doorway.

'She was great, wasn't she?' Angie turned to smile at her husband.

Stuart Boyd nodded. 'Excellent. But

I've come to take your pupil away, I'm afraid. I have an urgent memo I need to dictate.'

Liz got to her feet. 'I can't believe I just did that!'

Angie beamed at her. 'You see, I told you it wasn't as terrifying as you imagined it to be. Next time you come, you'll feel a lot more relaxed, won't you?'

★   ★   ★

'Liz, would you please try and relax?'

'But this is much more terrifying than making my first radio announcement.' Liz frowned. 'Rob, could it be that I'm just not cut out to be a driver?'

'Not at all. All you need do is stop looking down at the gear stick and keep your eyes on the road.'

'Thank goodness we're not on a real road,' she said, gazing out at the deserted airfield. 'So this place hasn't been used since the Second World War?'

'Occasional light aircraft land and

take off, but I checked with the man in charge and he assured me there'd be no activity here today. No planes, anyway!'

'Does everyone do as badly as me on their first attempt?'

Rob hesitated.

Liz groaned. 'I knew it!'

'Hey, I can't speak for everyone. I gave one of my sisters her first lessons, but she'd been longing to get behind the wheel and she'd watched how my father, then me, drove the family car, up until she had her seventeenth birthday and applied for a provisional licence.'

'Unlike me. My dad suggested I get my provisional licence and said he'd go through the basics with me, then treat me to lessons with a driving school. But this job came up.'

'You do have your licence? It doesn't matter here, but once we get on the public highway it's a must for a learner.'

'Don't worry, it's all dealt with. But it's probably going to be a while before you let me loose on a proper road.'

'We'll see about that. Now, tell me what you need to do before you press that ignition button.'

Liz couldn't believe how Rob could be so patient. She felt totally inept, whereas at least with Angie the day before, she'd not made too bad an attempt at sounding professional. And to think she'd considered that bank of switches and dials to be terrifying! This growling monster, whose engine she'd stalled twice so far, presented much more of a challenge. There was so much to think about; and how was she supposed to co-ordinate her feet and hands and look through the windscreen while not forgetting to check her mirrors?

But with Rob's gentle encouragement and a couple of false starts, next time she put the vehicle into first gear and released the hand brake, Liz drove forward smoothly, accelerator and clutch pedals doing what they should while she changed gear and, feeling the car's motion change, began bowling along.

'Um, maybe you could slow down a

bit, Liz. You don't have to drive like Stirling Moss,' said Rob.

Horrified, she checked the speedometer and discovered she was driving at twenty-five miles an hour. How frightening was that? At once she slackened speed.

'Listen to your engine,' said Rob. 'It's telling you to change down a gear.'

'Ooh,' said Liz. 'Is that all right?'

'Pretty darned good,' he said. 'Now, follow that track to your right or we'll reach the end of the runway, and I don't intend to cover reverse gear just yet.'

Liz learnt the true meaning of the expression 'kangaroo petrol' during her hour's instruction. She also realised what a powerful weapon she controlled whilst behind the wheel. At one point she almost cried with frustration when she steered off course and Rob called out, 'Whoa — where are you taking us now?'

She made it back to where they'd begun and brought the vehicle to a standstill. 'I hope I haven't ruined your engine or stripped the gearbox, whatever that means.' She turned to him.

'I don't think so,' he said. 'Now, how about I buy you lunch?'

She pulled a face. 'I've taken up enough of your time, Rob. It's very kind of you, but you really don't need to.' She opened her door and extricated herself from the driving seat, wishing, not for the first time, that she hadn't worn a stiff petticoat beneath her cotton skirt.

Rob opened the passenger door and unfolded his long legs before turning to face her. 'Well, I for one am ravenous, and unless you have other plans, it would be my pleasure to take you to lunch. There's a lovely old pub just down the road from the airfield. I can drop you off wherever you wish, after we've eaten.' He paused. 'The rest of the day is my own, so I'm happy to chauffeur you to one of the local beauty spots, if that appeals.'

She didn't quite know how to

answer. The great Rob Douglas, holiday camp heartthrob, was asking her out to lunch, despite the jerky ride his clumsy novice driver had inflicted on him. The open admiration in his eyes at once worried and delighted her. She'd wondered whether he had more than an hour's tuition in mind when he suggested changing his day off to coincide with hers.

This was probably a turning point in their relationship. Did she want to keep things on a friendly basis? Yes, of course she did; and why wouldn't friends decide to have lunch together, given neither of them had pressing engagements? Maybe she should invent an imaginary one for the evening. But she was being presumptuous, surely? He was unlikely to want her company for the whole of the day.

She made up her mind. 'Lunch would be lovely, Rob, but I insist on buying both our meals. You won't accept any petrol money, so please let me have my way. Please?'

Rob didn't immediately respond. He

didn't want to irritate Liz by turning down her offer, but his sister had told him time after time that not all girls liked to be put upon a pedestal, their every whim catered to. She'd also warned him about rushing into a relationship and risking putting off the object of his affections by being too generous. It had happened to him once before in his life, and Rob hoped he'd learned his lesson the hard way.

His background was a secure and wealthy one. He came from a long line of landowners, and his family home stood in acres of ground in Leicestershire. The only person at Rainbows who knew about this was Stuart Boyd, a person whom Rob greatly respected and trusted not to blow his cover. But who, he wondered, would in fact believe the story? It was pretty implausible to think someone like him, with the burden of expectation on his shoulders, chose to put on a snazzy uniform and spend his working hours helping others to party.

Liz was gazing at the old control tower. Maybe, like him, she was picturing those brave young pilots preparing to take to the skies in defence of their country. The whole atmosphere of the airfield seemed steeped in history, and Rob kept meaning to visit the local museum and see what information he could find. He was the possessor of an enquiring mind, and he had a hunch Liz might share this character trait.

From the snippets of information she'd revealed, he knew her parents lived in a modest house, and she'd attended the local grammar school and gone on to secure a secretarial qualification. He daren't reveal his academic background, though she'd probably never believe the product of a public school education could choose to work for Rainbows Holiday Camps. But then, that applied to his father, who wanted Rob to take over the family estate one day and couldn't understand how his son wished to follow his heart and devote himself to helping people enjoy their hard-earned holidays. Rob couldn't see how it should be claimed as wrong for someone to 'waste an education', as his father had warned. How could any education be wasted? And anyway, his old man would probably live to a ripe old age, so there was plenty of time to worry about the estate's future.

Now he had more than his job on his mind. He had lovely Liz filling his thoughts and his dreams. She was sometimes a little cool with him, and how refreshing he found that. Somehow he would convince her his intentions were purely honourable. Rob smiled to himself. It sounded as if he was about to ask for her hand in marriage. The warm feeling this thought produced surprised him, but no way would he let Liz suspect what absorbed him.

'Sorry, Liz,' he said, taking his car key from her outstretched hand. 'I was far away, thinking of all the aircrew who've flown in and out of here.'

'Or flown out and not returned,' she murmured.

'Hey, we mustn't get maudlin, though I would like to know more about the airfield's history. Loads of those airmen and women would've been the same age as you and me, some of them even younger.'

Liz nodded, taking her place in the passenger seat. 'I know. Maybe there's a museum in the nearest town.' She hesitated. 'I'm not sure where you plan on taking me for lunch, but please don't forget what I said.'

Rob got back behind the wheel. 'If it makes you happier, I'll let you pay. Is that all right?'

'Perfect.'

'Aha! That means I shall owe you another lunch another time.'

'No, it doesn't.' She put on a stern expression.

'We'll see about that. Now, I think there's a museum over at Coldmouth. That's only about five miles from The Old Bell, which is where I plan on taking you. But I mustn't monopolise your day.'

'Now you're talking like I was talking.' Liz chuckled. 'It sounds as if we have an interest in common, and I haven't yet visited Coldmouth, though I must say it doesn't sound too welcoming.'

'I've been there once or twice, and it's not a bad little town.' He switched on the engine. 'Um, now how does this gear thing work? Any idea, Aunty Liz?' Hastily he ducked as she flapped a hand at him.

★　★　★

The pub lunch had exceeded even Rob's expectations, and they'd just about managed to recover in time to explore the high street and find the museum, which was small but comprehensive. Liz made it clear she had letters to write later, deciding this would save him from any awkwardness about whether he ought to spend the evening with her. She'd bought some cake and fruit earlier as, although she could have made the first sitting in the dining room, she didn't need another cooked meal.

She let herself into the chalet, closing the door, her mind still revisiting some of the wartime anecdotes and photographs she'd seen earlier with Rob. Turning around, she jumped at sight of a figure curled up on the other bed.

The figure sat up. 'Hiya, Liz. I hope I didn't give you too much of a shock.'

'Goodness, Jenny, never mind that. It's lovely to see you again.' Liz watched the other girl smile and knew there was some sadness behind it.

'It's good to be back, and nice to see you too of course. How have you been getting on?'

'Not too bad, thanks.' Liz dropped her purchases on her bed and sank down beside them, kicking off her high-heeled sandals. 'I've had today off, but I think I need another one so I can recover.'

Jenny laughed. 'What have you been up to, may I ask?'

Liz hesitated. She'd enjoyed herself, but didn't fancy prattling on about her car-driving exploits and the delicious lunch and fascinating museum visit while Jenny was probably far more exhausted from her long train journey.

'This and that,' she said. 'More importantly, how are you, Jenny? And have you collected your mail yet?'

'I'm fine. I'll explain my mysterious absence in a while — but why the concern about my mail? Is this to do with something official from the boss?'

'Please don't look so worried. Stuart will be delighted to see you back, but I guess you've already been in touch?'

'Mmm. Not until last night, though. I rang Angie at their home, knowing he and you wouldn't be in the office at that time. I needed to tie up one final detail over my mum's care, but everything's in place now, thank goodness.'

Liz rose and went across to join her friend. She put her arm around Jenny's shoulders. 'I wondered if it was something to do with your mother, but Stuart didn't say a word. Hopefully I managed to bat off people's questions about where you were by saying you were dealing with an important family matter.'

'Thank you.' Jenny swallowed hard. 'When I set off that morning, I'd had a letter from Mum saying she'd received some rather bad news from her doctor. The letter had sat in my pigeonhole until I finished in the ballroom, and you were asleep when I got in. You can imagine all I had on my mind was getting home to her as soon as possible. I didn't even think of packing my case.'

'You didn't even take your toilet bag! That convinced me you hadn't planned on staying away.'

'I have plenty of summer clothes at home. What would be the point of bringing them when we work a six-day week?' Her eyes twinkled as she glanced at Liz's bulging curtain, behind which her clothes hung on a rail. 'I imagine when you packed it didn't cross your mind you'd end up wearing blue and white.'

'If I'd only known, I could have travelled a whole lot lighter.' Liz knew she sounded rueful. 'But it's great to be wearing a Rainbows uniform, even if I don't deserve that privilege.'

'Don't be daft.' Jenny checked her watch. 'Now that you've set me wondering, I'm definitely going to collect my mail. D'you fancy coming with me?'

'But you haven't told me about your mum yet.'

'No, but how about we stop off for a coffee on the way back? Unless you're off out somewhere again — maybe you've found yourself a boyfriend while my back's been turned?'

'Not really. Well, there's someone who . . . He's being very kind to me, and . . . '

'And you're blushing! Come on, Liz, you have to tell me more.'

Liz stood up. 'I need to get out of

these clothes and into some slacks and a blouse.'

'I'll allow that, but only if you tell me who you've been seeing. I bet I can guess, anyway.'

'Don't be silly! I bet you can't.'

'All right then — Rob's the one, isn't he?'

Liz stared at her. 'How on earth did you know?'

Jenny smirked. 'He'd hardly known you five minutes before he started going all gooey-eyed if ever your name came up in conversation. That's how I know.'

'Oh dear. Are you having me on?'

'Of course not. And I think it's lovely. Rob needs some stability in his life, though he certainly didn't hang about, did he?'

'Now don't go making a big thing of this. We're just friends, you know. Rob hasn't even kissed me yet! He asked me out for a meal while you were away, and today he's given me my first driving lesson.'

'And?' Jenny, having pushed her bare

feet into a pair of flip-flops, was rummaging in a drawer. She produced a comb and began tidying her hair in front of the only mirror the chalet offered.

'And we had a lovely lunch. I insisted on paying for both of us, so you needn't roll your eyes like that.'

'I shan't tease you, Liz. I'm a little surprised you haven't had that first kiss, though.'

'I can't think why.'

Jenny swung round. 'I wouldn't have thought Rob Douglas was backward in coming forward, that's all. So tell me why you were so quick to ask me whether I'd checked for mail.'

Liz stared at her friend, wondering how best to break the news of her old flame's reappearance.

'What's up, Liz? It can't be that difficult, surely?'

7

Summertime Blues

The two women decided to buy milkshakes instead of coffees, and chose a table inside the café as most customers were sitting outside. Jenny pulled the letter she'd opened so hurriedly from her shoulder bag and scanned the two sheets of notepaper once again. When she glanced up, Liz saw tears in her eyes.

'Are you all right? I hope he hasn't written anything to upset you.'

Jenny laughed. 'Far from it! I'm very touched, but oh my gosh, I can't believe Mike's tracked me down after all this time.'

Liz twirled the drinking straw around in her glass of creamy pink froth. 'Believe me, he sounded sincere. I had a shock when he first asked me for a dance because I suddenly realised I knew him from somewhere, though the cogs didn't quite settle in the right places. I was in pigtails and short socks when I last saw Mike Parks, so I'm amazed he recognised me.'

'He says in the letter that your hair gave you away, then your name badge triggered the memory. He also said you were very cagey about giving information, and that's why he trusted you enough to confide in you.'

Liz noted the way her friend's eyes took on a dreamy quality.

'I convinced myself Mike and I had no future together,' said Jenny. 'I'd already decided the military life wasn't for me; I didn't fancy the idea of being a soldier's wife, with all those long absences. I suppose I convinced myself I'd made the right decision for both of us.'

'But?'

Jenny leaned forward and rested her chin on her clasped hands. Liz hastily rescued the tall milkshake glass.

'I need to see him again, Liz — and

as soon as possible, don't you think? After all, the poor fellow might change his mind completely once he sees me for real. At the moment I only exist in his memory and he in mine.' She screwed up her face. 'Ooh, if only I hadn't been away while he was staying at the camp.'

'The main thing is, he's found you.'

'Yes. He says he'll travel back and stay overnight in a guesthouse, if I say the word. He's written his phone number underneath his address.' Jenny smiled wistfully. 'It's going to seem odd speaking to him again after all this time, but I can't wait to get in touch.'

'Will you arrange something on your next day off?'

'I hope so. I can hardly ask Stuart for extra time off, now can I?'

'So the reunion will take place next week?'

'I'll speak to Stuart tomorrow and explain why I'm so eager to confirm my next day off. I'll say an old friend wants to visit me.'

'Well, that's true enough.'

'I know; but this meeting is going to be a very significant one, Liz. I need to think hard about my own feelings, but I can't help but wonder whether I shouldn't just let things be. Wouldn't it be awful if one of us wanted to rekindle the friendship and the other didn't?' She folded her letter and put it back in her bag.

'Jenny, you worry too much. I think you owe it to Mike to go ahead and meet him, especially as he's prepared to come to you. He's not asking you to meet him halfway between here and wherever he lives now.'

'He's back living with his parents until he starts college in the autumn. He reckons he's going to enjoy being a mature student.'

Liz chuckled. 'It's funny to think of his mum and dad still living in that house. I can remember it as well as I remember the one we lived in.'

'Life's strange, isn't it? It's thrown you and me together, and if Mike hadn't turned up here I'd never have known we had a mutual friend.'

'That's how you should go on thinking about him, Jenny. What existed between you two is back in the past. If there's still a spark there, you'll soon know it.'

'Let's hope you're right. But Mike will be doing his teacher training course for the next three years, and well, I'm not. Unless I blot my copybook, the company could invite me back here next season, or possibly offer me a job in another location.' She sighed.

'So that's how it works?'

'Kind of. I've got several years' experience under my belt, so like Rob, I have a chance to make my way in the organisation. Your boss started out as a Rainbow host. That's how he met Angie, of course.'

'I see. I keep forgetting to ask what everyone does in the winter months. My mother's fretting already about my job prospects after September.'

'It depends on what people's talents are. Rainbow camps are all situated on the coast, so a small proportion of the summer staff are asked if they'd like to work on during the winter. That way the company can publicise weekend musical events and offer special rates to pensioners' clubs and retired service personnel organisations. Local people can book the ballroom for a big function, and entertainers and bands are brought in. Then of course there are things like building maintenance, catering and so on.'

'It's odd to think of the ballroom being decorated for Christmas, but of course it makes good business sense.'

'Anyway, thanks, Liz, for dealing with my old boyfriend so well.' Jenny held up her hand. 'No protests. I'm thankful you're the first person he approached, after spending the first couple of days trying to spot me.'

Liz was fighting hard not to yawn. 'I shan't protest; but if I don't drink up my milkshake and get off to bed soon, you're going to have to call out one of the camp trains to carry me there!'

★ ★ ★

Liz was in a thoughtful mood the next morning as she headed for the entertainments centre. She couldn't help dwelling on Jenny's comment that she and Rob hadn't yet shared a kiss. He hadn't wasted any time in asking her out, and he seemed to enjoy spending time with her. Why else would he have offered to teach her some driving techniques? But given her opinions about rushing things, wasn't it better this way? Keeping this new relationship on a friendly basis was what she wanted, wasn't it?

Maybe that was what Rob wanted, too. Perhaps she'd over-egged the pudding when it came to those imagined tender glances and wistful little smiles. Maybe Rob had had the image of a woman with blonde hair in his head, and she fitted this picture, although she wasn't quite the girl of his dreams.

She was on the phone to Rainbow

Command, as Stuart always referred to the holiday company's London office, when the object of her earlier thoughts tapped on her open door and gave her his wonderful lopsided smile as she glanced up from her notepad.

She covered the phone's mouthpiece with her spare hand. 'If you're looking for Stuart, he's on the other line. I'm just waiting for Mr Rainbow's secretary to confirm something.'

'Name-dropper,' he teased.

She shook her head at him. As soon as she'd received the information she needed and noted the details, Liz put down the phone.

'She was really friendly, Rob. I thought someone working for the big boss might be a bit snooty, but she knew I hadn't been in my job for long and asked me how I liked working here. I'm impressed.'

'It's one of the things I enjoy about being part of this organisation,' said Rob. 'As a young man, Joshua Rainbow had a dream, and he was determined to make it come true. He knows what it's like to put in long hours, so he makes sure our working conditions are as pleasant as possible. Oh, I know the company sometimes expects rather too much of us; but if you want to climb the ladder, you're encouraged to do so.'

'I doubt that could happen in my case,' said Liz.

'Why do you say that?'

'Don't get me wrong; I love my job, and it's a pleasure to come to work. But I have no illusions about what will happen come September.'

He frowned. 'I don't understand. I know you said your mother was concerned about you giving up a steady job to take a summer one, but you seemed happy enough about it.'

She stared at him, knowing she wasn't making sense. How on earth could she confess something that hadn't fully dawned on her until just now, when Rob Douglas had knocked on her office door and she'd glanced up at him? Her mouth had dried, and she felt the world tip on its axis! At that moment, if Rob told her he was going to work in the Rainbow camp situated furthest north of all, she would feel as though the bottom had dropped out of her world.

They were staring at one another as Stuart Boyd appeared behind his chief host. 'Sorry to keep you waiting, Rob. I imagine my secretary's been entertaining you.'

To Liz's horror, her boss sounded amused. She cleared her throat. 'Mr Rainbow's secretary has confirmed that date for your meeting with him, Stuart.'

'Excellent. You'll put it in my diary, won't you?'

'Of course.'

He turned to Rob. 'Please make sure your day off doesn't coincide with my trip to London, Rob. You know I don't like both you and I being away from the camp for more than a couple of hours while the Rainbows are on parade.'

'I'll write the date down for Rob, shall I?' Liz found a scrap of paper.

'Hey, my memory's not that bad.' Rob shot her a mischievous glance.

'All right, then. It's a week on Tuesday,' said Liz.

'Our driving lesson day!'

'I'm sorry if my meeting with the company chairman threatens to interfere with your social life, Rob,' said Stuart, this time not looking at all amused.

Liz, well aware she was blushing, wished she could be whisked away like magic and returned when her office was empty.

'We'll cope,' said Rob.

He appeared to see the funny side of what Liz considered to be an embarrassing moment. As he followed the boss through the doorway, he turned round and gave her a wink. 'We need to talk,' he said.

She wasn't sure what he meant, and was left wondering until she heard footsteps approaching. Cathy, the dance troupe leader, arrived in her office to report that one of her dancers had twisted her ankle while in the swimming pool, and the resident nurse had said she needed to rest up for at least a couple of days. Cathy was anxious to know whether Liz could juggle the schedule to allow for this.

Things didn't get better, and that afternoon Liz needed to take over from Angie in the radio studio while the presenter went home to sort out a domestic mishap. When Liz spotted Rob standing outside of her glass cage, she knew she must concentrate, and purposely didn't look in his direction.

But after she finished her announcement and looked back again, he had disappeared, as though he'd thought better of calling in. She hoped she hadn't upset him by not acknowledging his presence, but surely he of all people would know the importance of professionalism when it came to the Rainbow Radio broadcasts?

The rest of the day flew by. When Liz arrived at the dining hall in time for the evening meal, Rob was standing just outside the entrance. And for the first time ever, her heart missed a beat; not through longing, but because she thought he was looking at her as if she were a stranger.

'If I'm treading on some other fellow's toes, just say the word, Liz. I'm actually rather surprised at you, as well as being disappointed.'

She froze. 'I'm sorry, Rob, but I haven't a clue what you're talking about.'

'Really? I hate gossip — this place is alive with it — but when it comes to being made a fool of, I sit up and take notice of what's being said.'

'Hang on — is this what you meant when you said we needed to talk? Are you accusing me of something?'

'When I said that, I meant we should work out a schedule for your next few driving sessions.' He hesitated. 'But if the cap fits — '

Liz pursed her lips. 'I wish you'd come out with whatever's bugging you. Until you do, this conversation's going nowhere.'

He clenched his fists at his sides. 'I think it's fair to say you've given me the impression that you welcomed my attentions.'

'Rob, you sound as if you've stepped straight out of *Pride and Prejudice*. What's going on?'

He ran his fingers through his hair. 'Oh, I know I was a bit quick off the mark in asking you out, but you could've said no. Since I left my chalet this morning, I've discovered you have some other fellow in your life. You caused tongues to wag in the ballroom, so I'm told.'

'Here you go again! If this is about what I think it's about, your informant definitely got hold of the wrong end of the stick.'

He sighed and studied his feet. 'There was more than one informant, Liz, but I shouldn't have tackled you about this with so many people around. For that I apologise. Anyway, I'm not in the mood to discuss this further just now.' He stuck his hands in his pockets and met her gaze. 'Perhaps you'd like to get your story straight, because I'm coming to the office for a meeting with Stuart and Colin tomorrow morning and I intend to ask you one simple question, to which I expect a truthful reply.' With that, he pushed open the door and waited for her to precede him.

Liz took a deep breath. How dare he speak to her like that! How dare he state his terms in such a way? But she didn't trust herself to make any further comment.

And it took a tremendous effort to paste a smile on her face when she approached her rapidly-filling-up table of holidaymakers. How swiftly that fluffy pink cloud she'd so recently been floating upon had dissolved, only to send her spinning into deep dejection.

8

The Naughty Lady of Shady Lane

'You were restless last night!' Jenny raised her head from her pillow.

'Oh Jenny, I'm sorry if I disturbed you, but it took ages for me to drop off. I can't tell you how many sheep I counted.'

'It's okay; I think I'd have lain awake anyway, thinking, wondering — no prizes for guessing why, of course.'

'Did you speak to Stuart about your day off?'

'I did, and he was fine about it. So I bit the bullet, and before I did my ballroom stint I used the phone box outside reception to ring Mike.'

'I can imagine he'd have been on tenterhooks waiting to hear from you.'

'Yes; I wouldn't have wanted to put him through a long wait, after all the trouble he'd gone to.'

'Come on then, do you two have a plan?'

Jenny chuckled. 'We do. Both of us agreed we need to meet and see how we feel about each other. This must be one of the strangest romances in history, don't you think?'

'I'm not saying a word, but I'll be crossing my fingers you make the right decision, Jen.'

Jenny watched Liz pick up her toilet bag and towel. 'Are you sure you're all right? That problem you had getting to sleep — you haven't fallen out with Rob, have you?'

'Not at all.' Liz lifted her chin. 'Although it appears he's fallen out with me.'

'Oh no. Is there anything I can do? I hate seeing you look so woebegone. You were all sparkly and lovely after I got back and you came into the chalet. I felt quite envious.'

'Was it so very obvious?' Liz sank onto her bed again. 'Oh Jenny, it's crazy to fall for someone in such a rush when we both know so little about each other. I've tried to keep our friendship as . . . well, as just platonic, but — '

'Yep. The absence of a first kiss would indicate that.' Jenny nodded.

'Well, that would be up to Rob, wouldn't it? I'm not that emancipated a woman! And I've been thinking lately that he and I had reached a point where we might share our feelings about one another.'

'And has that happened, dare I ask?'

'Huh! After the way we parted company last night, I doubt very much whether he'll bother even looking at me again.'

'I didn't realise things had got that bad. But what on earth's been happening to you both?'

'Rob has been listening to gossip, that's what. He seems to think I'm some kind of flirt.'

'But that's ridiculous! For a start, it's obvious you're not that sort of girl. And besides, you have hardly any spare time for getting into mischief, even if you wanted to.'

'Nor energy! Look, please don't take this the wrong way, as Rob so obviously has, but that evening when Mike came up to me in the ballroom, I had more than one dance with him.'

'I know about that because he told me in his letter. So what?'

'I was in blue and white, that's what. And I totally forgot I shouldn't dance too many times with the same holiday-maker. By the time I noticed two or three people glaring at me, the damage must've been done.'

'Ah, I understand now. So Rob's got wind of this and he's added up two and two to make five.'

'I'm afraid so. In Rob's mind I'm being wooed by a handsome stranger, and he's decided people must be laughing behind his back.'

Liz noticed Jenny's cheeks turning a becoming shade of pink. 'Yes, the Mike I remembered has turned into a very attractive man, Jen. When Cathy whisked him away to dance, she seemed very taken.'

'Thanks for the warning.' But Jenny was smiling. 'Luckily for me, Cathy has a steady boyfriend.'

'And I met Mike for coffee next morning and agreed to pass on a letter to you, so it's possible someone noticed us in the café. I asked Angie's advice, you know. That's how careful I was about your privacy. Angie could easily vouch for me and put paid to Rob's suspicions.'

'But why don't I sort this out, Liz?' Jenny snuggled back under her counterpane. 'When I see Rob, I'll explain exactly who that handsome stranger was and why you were spending time with him. After all, this misunderstanding is, in a way, my fault.'

'In his current mood, I suspect Rob mightn't believe you, Jen. I think he'll assume you're telling fibs because I've asked you to help me pull the wool over his eyes. I wouldn't be surprised if he thought I was sucking up to him because he's teaching me to drive.'

'That's nonsense. I can convince him you're not the kind of girl who'd two-time a fellow. Don't worry about it.'

Liz stood up. 'I feel so hurt — not to mention being angry with him, never mind disappointed that he's listened to rumours rather than let me state my case. You should've heard the high-handed way he told me he was coming into the office this morning and intended to ask me one question.'

She stared at her friend. 'I refuse to let him treat me like this, Jenny. Rob's ruined my trust in him, and all because he's more interested in what other people think than in hearing my side of the story. Please, please don't mention anything to him, even though I know you mean well. He's proved what he thinks of me deep down. And his opinion is a pretty poor one.'

Liz fled before the tears flowed. On her way to her ablutions, she willed herself not to become so upset that she couldn't face going into work. And there was breakfast to get through. She needed at least a cup of tea and some toast before tackling another hectic morning.

After a quick bath and shampoo, Liz towel-dried her hair and brushed it, leaving it loose so it framed her face. She hurried back to the chalet to get dressed and found Jenny either fast asleep again, or pretending to be. No matter. The second-sitting wake-up music would eventually rouse her in time for breakfast.

Liz smoothed down her pleated skirt, pushed her feet into white shoes and let herself out into the sunny morning. She kept her head down, hoping she wouldn't cross Rob's path on her way to the dining hall. This was what she'd feared all along — the possibility of starting something which, when it finished, would cause both of them embarrassment, let alone the pain of rejection. But she hadn't anticipated the sudden end to a relationship hardly begun.

'Hey, honeybun, you're looking even more delectable than usual this morning,' Harry, the camp comic, said as he fell into step with her.

She glanced sideways at him. 'You're so good for my morale, Harry.'

'Hmm, eyes a little puffy, though. Your beautiful countenance somewhat pale. Boyfriend trouble, is it? I gather there are rivals for the fair lady's hand.'

Liz stopped walking. 'Not you as well, Harry. I can't believe this place! Anyone would think I was a scarlet woman.'

'Poor Liz.' He patted her shoulder. 'We'd better get a move on or everyone else will be wolfing down our share of the eggs and bacon. Just remember, Miss Liz Lane — you're a delightful young lady and you're already a popular Rainbow, but there are jealous folk on the staff, and if that young whippersnapper believes them over you, then he darned well doesn't deserve you anyway!'

'Why would anyone be jealous of me?

I'm nothing special, and it's not like Rob and I are even going steady.'

'He's head over heels, anyone can see that.'

'So I've been told.' Liz sighed. 'Not anymore though.'

'It's none of my business, I know.'

'Oh, don't mind me, Harry. No one else appears to.'

They paused at the dining hall entrance. Liz felt a pang as she realised Harry was standing precisely where Rob stood the previous evening to deliver his bombshell.

'I hate to see you unhappy, sweetheart. But if the man's wronged you, then you should tell him so. Stand up for yourself. And if he's daft enough to let you go, there are always plenty more fish in the sea.'

Liz nodded. Harry meant well, but she really wasn't interested in any other fish.

'Now go tuck into breakfast and remember what your Uncle Harry told you.'

* ★ ★

At half-past nine, reception rang to tell Liz a bouquet of flowers had been delivered for her. Her heart tried to escape her ribcage as her resolve almost melted, until her brain took charge and sent a stern message to that most tender and wilful of organs.

'Um, I — are you sure there hasn't been some mistake?' she quizzed the receptionist.

'The label says Miss Elizabeth Lane, secretary to the entertainments manager, Rainbow Holidays, South Bay. That is you, isn't it?'

'Yes. I'll collect them as soon as I can.'

Liz replaced the receiver, wishing she could have refused to take delivery of flowers that could only have been ordered by one person. Yet that action would have surely fuelled further speculation about her. Although the happy campers were replaced by a new crowd each Saturday, the resident staff soon got to know other people working in the same department, and those most under the spotlight were the Rainbow hosts and hostesses. Even though Liz had arrived at the camp later than all the others, she hadn't taken long to realise how quickly the jungle drums could start beating.

She glanced at her watch. She might as well go to the mailroom and collect the post before picking up the flowers. Angie was on duty that morning, so she'd present the bouquet to her. And if Rob asked whether she'd received it, she'd jolly well tell him she wasn't going to be bought off by gifts. So there!

★　★　★

The pink carnations and rosebuds smelt heavenly. Liz, having rummaged in the stock room, found a glass vase and filled it at the washbasin in the ladies' room. Angie got up and opened the door to her studio as she spotted her visitor approaching.

'What's this?' The announcer's eyes twinkled. 'I'm sure it isn't my birthday or our wedding anniversary.'

Liz laughed. 'Maybe you have a secret admirer.'

'Seriously, Liz — that man of mine is a sweetheart, but he's only ever bought me flowers when I've announced a forthcoming happy event! And I think I'd know if I was expecting again. So please tell me what all this is about before the disc that's playing comes to an end.'

Liz bit her lip. 'You'll be doing me such a favour by accepting them, Angie. Someone's sent them to me, and that person could be Rob — in which case, believe me, I can't bear them near me, lovely as they are.'

Angie buried her nose among the fragrant petals. 'Mmm, they certainly smell heavenly, but leave them here if it makes you feel better. Frankly, I haven't a clue what Rob's done to make you feel like you do.'

'You must be about the only person on the entertainments staff who doesn't. If anyone's name is mud, it's mine.'

Angie looked puzzled. 'I don't get out much, as you know. This glass cage is a barrier in more ways than one. And Stuart's hopeless at knowing what's going on when it comes to affairs of the heart.'

'That's a relief. I'd hate to blot my copybook with him too.'

Angie glanced at the clock. 'I must get back to my seat. Come to think of it, the other day Stuart did say something about you and Rob maybe being a little more than just good friends.'

'I thought the same.' Liz sighed. 'Look, Angie, I promise to explain it to you some other time.' She recalled Harry's advice. 'I think it's important you know the score, as it's kind of tied up with Jenny and her friend Mike.'

'Goodness, so the plot thickens. All right, my dear, I'll pop in when I finish my shift.'

Liz arrived at her desk moments

ahead of Colin, who didn't seem to want to meet her eye. Her heart plummeted. 'Oh Colin, not you as well.'

'I don't like to see Rob so miserable,' he muttered.

'And how do you think I feel?'

He met her gaze. 'I don't know; you tell me. The word is that some lucky holidaymaker swept you off your feet while Rob's back was turned, though I must say I'm surprised to hear it. I thought you and he were made for each other.'

'Colin, I can assure you there is no romance with a holidaymaker. Believe me, the only thing wrong that I have done was to dance too often with one of the campers.'

'I remember. That was the night I tried to remind you of the rules, though you seemed rather too preoccupied with your partner.'

'There was a good reason for it, but I refuse to disclose private matters that don't concern you or Rob or any other Tom, Dick or Harry! Get it?'

'Yes, ma'am.' Colin looked suitably shameful. 'I apologise if I've spoken out of turn. You do a good job, Liz, and I value you as a friend; but I feel I've been placed in an awkward position.'

Liz nodded. His kind words touched her, but she knew that his friendship with Rob had formed long before she had come on the scene, and that was where his loyalties lay.

'Colin, did you by chance mention anything to Rob about seeing me in the ballroom? He wasn't there that evening, but someone's been mischief-making.'

'Well, it's not me, Liz. I'd never stir things up like that.'

'I thought as much. Thanks, Col. I wish I knew who told him, though.'

Beyond the glass partition behind Colin, Liz saw Rob appear in the corridor.

She raised her voice but kept her gaze on Colin. 'Right, now you're both here, you're to go straight into Mr Boyd's office. Thank you.'

She sat down and opened her

shorthand notebook, trying to decipher squiggles that normally she transcribed into plainer English than her boss used when dictating. That was part of her role. But not this morning, not when the symbols blurred on the page and she felt as though the breath had been squeezed out of her. Her mouth was dry. She couldn't stop trembling. And she daren't look at Rob, even though she ached to run into his arms and hear him tell her this nasty situation was the result of a stupid mistake.

But that wasn't going to happen. He'd hurt her very deeply, and at that moment Liz couldn't help wishing she was back in her old office chasing up suppliers, typing boring letters, and wondering whether she possessed enough willpower to ignore the treacle sponge pudding lurking on the canteen's lunch menu.

But she was fooling herself. Hadn't she begun longing for change once she had her former job at her fingertips? She'd been thrilled to get the call from the entertainments manager after he'd shouted for help to head office. They'd forwarded her contact details to Stuart Boyd, and now the rest was history. Liz still loved her new position, but how could she fulfil her duties satisfactorily when every working day she was bound to bump into the chief Rainbow host?

Slowly she pulled herself together, and soon her fingers flew over the keyboard. Totally absorbed, she jumped when someone appeared in her doorway.

'Could we talk?' Rob paused. 'Please.'

She'd made up her mind. So she looked at him, aware her expression was what her mum would call stony-faced. 'No, actually we can't talk. Not now. Not later.'

'Will you at least allow me to apologise?'

He sounded contrite, and she longed to look at him, but steeled herself to keep gazing at her notebook.

'Liz?'

'Please leave now, Rob, unless of

course you need to give me an instruction from Mr Boyd.'

He groaned. 'For the love of Pete! You're not helping this situation, Liz. I'm sorry I spoke to you as I did yesterday. Please believe me — I was upset and angry, and . . . well, to be honest, not seeing things straight.'

'You behaved appallingly and without any reason at all. I made a mistake, but I was acting with the best of intentions.' Liz whirled round on her typist's chair so she faced him.

'What, by flirting in the ballroom, you mean?' He held both hands, palms upwards, in front of him. 'Can't you understand how hurtful it was for me to be told by two different people who saw you have several dances with a male camper, let alone two or three who saw you having coffee with him the next day?'

'Oh, loads of people must have seen me, Rob. Tell me, just how small-minded are these friends of yours? I can't believe I'm hearing this.'

'Maybe they care about me and thought I should be warned.'

She shook her head slowly. 'I could easily explain everything to you. I could give you the names of two or three people, each of them close to you, who'd back me up. But I have no intention of doing so. You preferred to listen to people blackening my character rather than come and talk to me. How could I ever have a close friendship with you with that standing between us?'

He took a step towards her. 'Liz, do you care for me at all? That's the one question I've been wanting to ask you.'

'Did you not understand what I just said, Rob? Surely there's nothing more to say?'

She saw a spasm cross his face. Then he turned on his heel and left her office. She heard the sound of his feet clattering down the stairs as she put her head in her hands and wondered if her world would ever again right itself.

9

Love Is Strange

Liz skipped lunch. Despite the sea air, her appetite had vanished, so she bought a couple of apples in the camp shop and hurried back to her chalet. On the threshold, she stopped as the heady fragrance of fresh flowers enveloped her.

To her surprise, on Jenny's bedside cabinet stood a similar arrangement to the one Liz had given away to Angie. But these flowers were yellow and cream, equally as beautiful as the pink ones, and giving off just as delicious a scent, as well as prompting Liz to wonder what on earth was going on.

She couldn't resist peering at the card lying beside the bouquet that Jenny, bless her, had arranged in a child's plastic beach bucket she'd filled with water. The words on the card read: *To Jenny. All my love, Mike.*

Liz turned away and sank down on her bed, still staring at the rosebuds and carnations. So that must mean Mike had sent each of them a bouquet, and the pink flowers were not after all from Rob. If she'd thanked Rob for them, he'd probably have stormed out of her office. If she'd placed them on her desk in full view of everyone, he'd probably have stormed out of her office. Liz wondered whether Jenny knew of Mike's kind gesture towards his sister's former school friend.

Liz groaned. She'd better explain her actions to her chalet mate, in case Jenny noticed the flowers in the Rainbow Radio studio and started making two and two add up to five, as certain people were prone to do lately. She couldn't afford to offend another of the few friends she'd made within the camp.

She was startled when a key turned in her door and Jenny came in.

'Hello, I don't often see you here during working hours.' Jenny peered at her friend. 'You look terrible.'

'Thanks a million.'

'I didn't mean to be rude, but it's obvious you're unhappy, Liz. You've seen Rob, I suppose?'

'I have. He wanted to apologise. What's more, if I hadn't been so angry, I'd have thanked him for sending me a bouquet I now suspect must have come from Mike.'

Jenny sat down opposite Liz. 'I came back for my swimming kit, but I can spare five minutes. I had a letter from Mike saying he'd ordered flowers for you too, as a thank-you.' She smiled. 'The old smoothie remembered how much I adore yellow rosebuds. The carnations are beautiful too.'

Liz knew her laugh sounded hollow. 'At least someone's pleased with me. Rob was trying to apologise, but all the soft soap in the world won't put things right between us.'

'Have you put Mike's flowers in your

office?' She narrowed her eyes. 'Oh, no, don't tell me Rob saw them and jumped to the wrong conclusion!'

'It's all right. I gave them to Angie after I collected them from reception. Mike's message must have got lost somehow.'

'I see. Well, I'm sure Angie won't mind if you take them back. They're meant for you, after all.'

'It was very kind of Mike — and please pass my thanks to him, Jenny — but I think I'd better leave things as they are. This whole business is becoming too complicated.' Liz picked up an apple and polished it against her blue blazer.

'I do wish you'd let me explain everything to Rob. I don't suppose you'd — '

'No. Whatever it is, I wouldn't.'

'You two remind me of the mountain and Mohammed.' Jenny rose and rummaged in the bottom of her wardrobe.

'Well, if certain people used their

common sense, life would be a great deal easier. As it is, I'm going to have to hand in my notice.'

'What did you say?' Jenny turned round, clutching a green bathing suit.

'Think about it, Jenny. Would you want to keep coming face to face with a man you really, really liked, and truly believed was fond of you? That's the same man you despise for not trusting you, but can't ignore because you need to co-operate with him and consult him as part of your daily job routine?'

'Why are you being so stubborn? I could bang your heads together, really I could.'

'No need. I intend to work out my notice, after which I won't be around to annoy anyone anymore.'

And as Jenny stared in dismay at her, Liz at last let down the barriers and sobbed as though her heart was broken, never to be mended.

★　★　★

'Stuart! I'm sorry to burst in on you like this, but something dreadful is about to happen.'

The entertainments manager looked up in surprise. 'Whatever's wrong, Jenny? This isn't about your mum, I hope?'

'No, it's about Liz. When she comes back from her lunch break, she intends to hand in her notice.'

'You're not serious?' He rose from his chair and came round his desk to pull up a chair for her.

'Thanks.' She sat down. 'I still feel a bit shaky. She's absolutely adamant she can't work here any longer.'

'I see. Well, actually I don't see, but I imagine you can explain to me what's going on.'

Jenny nodded. 'You probably know she and Rob have been seeing each other outside of working hours. And now, because of Liz's kindness in trying to help sort things out for me and my ex boy-friend, Rob's offended because someone told him she was flirting with

173

Mike while he was on holiday here. That's my Mike I'm talking about. Well, not mine exactly, but I'm hoping. Um, Mike's the man Liz danced with all those times in the ballroom last week — but only because he was looking for me.'

Stuart stared blankly back at her.

'Mike bumped into Liz and kind of recognised her because she used to be his sister's best friend years ago when they were in pigtails. Well, Mike wasn't, obviously, because he was in the army. So when he saw her name badge and asked her to dance, he introduced himself, and she — I mean Liz — remembered him. But when he asked if I still worked for Rainbows, she was quite rightly reluctant to give him any information in case I didn't want to see him again.'

Stuart took a large white handkerchief from his trouser pocket and wiped his forehead. Then he reached for the glass of water on his desk and drank from it. Deeply. 'Have you told Rob about all this?'

'Gosh, no. Liz would have my guts for garters if I did. I'm sworn to secrecy; so please, Stuart, don't tell her I've been to see you.' She glanced at her watch. 'I have to go. I'm due at the pool. Please can you do something about this?'

'I don't want to lose Liz, that's for sure, but I can't dictate to my secretary about her, erm, her decisions regarding male persons who are attracted to her.'

'I think those two fancy each other rotten!' Liz jumped up. 'So please, please, don't let her go.'

Stuart grimaced. 'This may sound selfish, but Liz has made life a lot easier for me and I'd hate to see her go. Angie's fond of her too.'

'I know! But because a couple of the Rainbows seem to be jealous of Liz, they've poisoned Rob against her; and even though he tried to apologise, she's decided she doesn't want to know him because he believed them rather than her.'

'I see. At least, I think I see. Cripes.'

Jenny heaved a sigh of relief. 'That's all right, then. I knew I could rely on you.' She jumped to her feet. 'I'm off now — I don't want to bump into Liz in case she suspects me of disobeying her orders. I do feel partly responsible for this, you know.'

Stuart nodded. 'I understand how you feel.'

Left alone, he put his head in his hands and thought. What would his wife suggest?

Five minutes later, when Liz turned up, she found no sign of her boss. She clicked her tongue in annoyance and walked down the corridor to her own office. If she couldn't inform Stuart face to face of her decision, she could at least write a brief letter confirming she was giving one week's notice of her intention to quit her job, as from that day. She set about her task at once, making sure she wrote down both the date and time of writing.

* * *

Rob was at the poolside, helping Colin chivvy children into groups, ready for the kiddies' swimming gala. Mums, dads, grandmas and grandpas sat in rows of striped canvas deck chairs on three sides. On seeing his boss approach, Rob wondered what was up. The entertainments manager was generally so busy juggling appointments and queries and fixing gigs with guest performers that he rarely made an appearance at routine weekly events so ably organised by the Rainbow hosts. The campers would have no idea who Stuart was, as he always wore a business suit, or slacks and a casual shirt if he wasn't involved in meetings.

As soon as the next race began, Stuart was at Rob's side. 'How do you fancy a change of scenery?'

'At the moment, it sounds very tempting. I'm afraid your secretary's furious with me,' said Rob.

'My secretary is about to hand in her notice.'

'What? Who said? We can't let her do that, Stuart.'

'Jenny tells me Liz has decided it's impossible for you and her to work together. The only way I think we can change her mind is for you to get away for a while. It's not a bad thing for you to work with one of the other managers; get a fresh perspective.'

'That's as may be, but how will you cope, a man down? You know we often have to spread the Rainbows thinly over the ground as it is.'

'I'm well aware of that. Without going into too much detail, I had a quick word with head office, and it appears the chief Rainbow at Seacliffe Camp is keen to gain experience at one of our bigger resorts.'

'That's Graham, isn't it? He's a nice fellow. So you're saying he and I would swap places?'

'On a short-term basis, anyway. At least that way we'd keep both you and Liz. Hopefully things would settle down and you and Graham could return to your own jobs.'

Rob grunted.

'It's arguably the best option,' said Stuart. 'I don't want to lose Liz, and I certainly don't want to lose you, but nor can I tolerate you and her being at loggerheads every time your paths cross.'

'We're not children,' said Rob, scowling into the distance.

'Agreed. But you are human, and I'd sooner you weren't placed in a difficult situation. So, shall I ring Seacliffe and set the wheels in motion?'

'Do I have any alternative?'

'Well, there is one I can think of. But first I need to know whether, if Liz can be persuaded to change her mind, you'd be willing to stay in your position on the same site as her.'

'Of course I would, Stuart. I'm learning a lot from you. I can't bear the thought of losing Liz either. I'll go down on my knees and beg her to forgive me, if it'll make her change her mind.'

'Maybe I can think of some more subtle means. But does this mean you're what some might call keen on the young lady?'

'Keen?'

Stuart sighed. 'This is much more my wife's area of expertise than mine, but she tells me I need to face facts. All right — do you, erm, love the girl?'

Rob stared at him. 'Yes. I didn't know how much I did, until she tore me off a strip. That's when I realised what a fool I'd been. And now Liz won't give me the time of day.'

'If push comes to shove, you might have to grovel a bit in order to convince her there's room for the pair of you here, where you both belong.' Stuart smiled wryly. 'I can at least try to stall her for the time being; somehow find a way not to accept her notice — that way she'll have more time to think and hopefully cool down. I'll get Angie on the case. She's aware of the situation, and Liz gets on well with my wife.'

'Liz gets on well with lots of people,' said Rob gloomily. 'I must have been out of my tiny mind, taking notice of spiteful gossip. What was I thinking of?'

'What indeed? But love does strange things to folk.'

★ ★ ★

Liz was typing up the next day's schedule of events when she glimpsed her boss walking past her office. He must either be going downstairs or going to call on Angie. Liz went on typing. A few minutes later, she saw him stalk past her office, eyes averted, on his way back. She picked up the white envelope propped against her pen and pencil jar and hurried next door.

'Come in,' called Stuart.

He wore such a grim expression that Liz hesitated to step further than the threshold.

'Well, what it is?' The remark was more of a snarl.

'Oh dear, have I chosen a bad moment?'

'You could say that. I'm faced with a staff crisis. I could well lose a highly valued member of my team, probably for good. In fact, it's very likely that will happen.

'Quite frankly, Miss Lane, coming so soon after the sordid episode when your predecessor ran away with one of my best Rainbow hosts, it makes me wonder whether all this upheaval in the team is worth the trouble of trying to keep this particular boat afloat.' He paused. 'I'd have a more peaceful life, driving a milk float.'

Liz stared at him, horrified. She'd turned back into Miss Lane! And what did Stuart mean when he mentioned a highly valued staff member? Surely Rob hadn't handed in his notice because of recent events? If that was the case, did her boss know what happened to upset Rob? Her tummy performed what swimming coach Colin would no doubt describe as a double back flip.

'So unless you come bearing glad tidings, I suggest you return to your post and finish typing tomorrow's schedule, after which perhaps you'd care to join me, while together we puzzle over who we can miraculously slot into the chief Rainbow Host's position in tomorrow's events, not forgetting we have two Rainbows on day off plus one hostess unavailable for her usual duties as she's still standing in for the dancer who hurt her ankle.'

So it really was Rob her boss was talking about. Liz sucked in her breath. Stuart's abrupt attitude towards her sent shivers down her spine.

'What is it?'

'You're telling me R — Rob is thinking of leaving?'

'Leaving this particular camp, yes indeed, although it seems some other site will be honoured by his services. I'm about to ring head office to see whether they can dust off their magic wand and find me a replacement.'

'I — I'd better get on then.'

Liz stumbled the short distance back to her desk. She sat down heavily on her chair and stared at the schedule, once more neatly written by Rob ready for her to type. So he'd beaten her to it. He'd asked for a transfer. Of course the organisation wouldn't want to lose him, not when they were quietly grooming him for stardom. Without a doubt, Rob was one of Stuart's blue-eyed boys and her boss was understandably devastated.

Her cheeks burned with shame. She'd been in her new job a matter of weeks and here she was, at the eye of the storm. Who would Stuart prefer to keep in the team? There was only one answer to that question. But she daren't delay her current task and cause any more upset.

She typed as fast as she could, stopping two or three times when she made an error and was forced to correct it. At last she completed her work but rather than face her boss just then, she headed for Rainbow Radio, where she knew Angie was reaching the end of her shift.

Liz hovered outside the door, listening to an announcement nearing its end. She watched Angie pick up the arm of the record player and hold it over the turntable ready to place it deftly on the next disc. Soon, the mellow sound of Jim Reeves singing *I Can't Stop Loving You* percolated through the loudspeaker system.

Liz swayed slightly. She took a deep breath, caught the presenter's eye through the glass partition and pushed open the door, closing it gently behind her.

'Yes?' Angie's voice was cool, businesslike and not at all welcoming as it usually was.

Bewildered by this chilly reception, Liz shook her head. 'My world's crashing all round me. I came for some advice.'

'Really? Well, I doubt you'll listen to advice, even if I offer it. When you let me in on what happened to make Rob so upset, you were very much of the opinion that you were in the right and he was wrong.'

'Angie, that's not fair! You know I

wouldn't have had this happen for all the tea in China. Can no one understand I'm upset too?'

'Sometimes pride has a lot to answer for.'

'From what Stuart said, it seems Rob wants to work elsewhere.'

'So I hear. No prizes for guessing how upset he is, Liz. In fact, both of them are. I hope you're pleased with yourself.'

Liz lifted her chin. 'So it's all my fault, is it?'

Angie shrugged. 'Only you can answer that.'

'Well, if it makes you feel any better, I've written out my notice, giving seven days, as from two o'clock this afternoon.'

'Oh, that's just great. What a pathetic thing to do. Let me tell you, Liz, how good a job you're doing. My husband's delighted with the way you've fitted in and, don't let this go to your head but Stuart says you're the best secretary he's ever had. He comes home in a much better mood these days. And here we are, only halfway through the season and you're chucking it in. So poor Stuart loses two of his best staff members in the same week. What the heck are you playing at?'

Liz stared at her. Angie didn't mince her words. Put like that, how could she possibly leave her boss in the lurch? Stuart and Angie had been more than kind and welcoming. Was this how she repaid them? Especially as she knew her predecessor had vanished without even handing in her notice. But how could she swallow her pride and tell Stuart she'd stay on, after the awful way she'd accused Rob of such bad behaviour?

'I'm sorry to have troubled you, Angie,' said Liz. 'You've been so kind to me, both you and your husband. I need time to think. It hadn't occurred to me how selfish I was being.'

'Yes, well, that's something to be thankful for, I suppose. You should at least sleep on it, Liz. And do give some thought to how this short stay in a new job is going to affect your career prospects. Hmm?'

★   ★   ★

When Liz left, Angie checked how much time remained before her current record choice ended. Swiftly she picked up the phone and dialled her husband's extension.

He picked up immediately. 'Stuart Boyd.'

'Hello, I've just had Liz in here. I think I handled her as we discussed we should.'

'I'm sure you did. How did she react?'

'Very bravely, but I could tell she was hurt by my lack of sympathy. It was awful seeing her standing there, obviously stunned by my frigid manner. And when she left the studio, her shoulders were drooping as if her world had ended. Oh, dear, I so wanted to give her a big hug and tell her everything would turn out right in the end.'

'I'm sure. Well, I'm not in the business of marriage brokering, but I don't want to see those two at loggerheads either. People pay good money to come and be entertained by happy hosts and hostesses!'

'Have you accepted Liz's notice?'

He chuckled. 'Fortunately she dropped the envelope while I was doing my grumpy boss act, and I was holding my breath when she left my office without realising she hadn't actually achieved what she came in for.'

'Really? So where's the letter now?'

'In my inside jacket pocket,' said Stuart. 'Let's hope I can rip it up before too long.'

'Better still, let's hope Liz asks you for it back so she can rip it up herself.'

'I live in hope. I certainly don't intend to open it.'

'I bet you wish those two had never fallen for each other in the first place, don't you?'

Her husband's warm chuckle trickling down the telephone made Angie smile.

'Not at all. I remember very vividly

what it was like when I realised I was falling in love with you,' said Stuart. 'These two are even younger than we were.'

'We fell out a couple of times too, don't forget.'

'But we'd known each other for almost the whole of that summer season before I plucked up the courage to ask you out.'

'Ah, but it was me who asked you out, don't you remember?'

'I thought our first date was that dinner and dance in the town hall. A little group of us went from the camp.'

'Yes, but I got invited because I was running their radio station and the entertainments manager asked me to choose one of the boys to be my escort for the evening. I chose you because I was getting fed up with waiting for you to ask me out.'

'My memory must be failing. But I'm glad your dastardly plan worked!'

Angie squealed down the phone. 'I gotta go. See you later, my love.' She flicked the magic switch. 'We're playing romantic songs this afternoon.' Deliberately she purred down the microphone. 'We've heard it once already but I've had a request to play it again. This one's for a camper called Stuart.'

She knew her wicked grin wouldn't be seen by anyone, but she reckoned everyone within easy distance of a loudspeaker would hear her announce a request only she knew was fictitious. As the gentle sounds of 'I Can't Stop Loving You' rolled around the camp, those listening would include her husband in his office, his secretary in her office, and hopefully the chief host.

Angie glanced at her copy of the schedule. At this time, Rob should be heading for the Buckingham Ballroom, ready to comperè the Gorgeous Grannies contest — so he couldn't help but listen to her crafty choice of record. Hopefully those two stubborn individuals would see sense before too much longer. Romance sometimes needed a little shove to help it along, and there was still time for Liz and Rob to kiss and make up.

10

I Can't Stop Loving You

Liz walked towards the dining hall, determined to keep a brave face on. Why, oh why had she been so reluctant to see Rob's side of the story? She'd been quick enough to accuse him of making up his mind too hastily and condemning her. If events were reversed and one or two people she knew well enough to trust mentioned to her that Rob was spending rather too much time with a young female holidaymaker, how might she react?

She needed time to think. It still rankled that he didn't know Jenny's story. Yet, having pleaded with Jenny not to explain things to Rob, Liz didn't feel able to back down. She could only hope she didn't bump into him on her way to her seat. If she could only get there before him — or after him — she could avert her eyes and pretend to have other things on her mind. But nothing else in the world was more important than putting a stop to this horrible icy barrier between the two of them.

She quickened her pace, falling into step with a couple whose seats were at Liz's end of the dining table. They were a pleasant pair, visiting the resort for the first time. She'd teased the husband about bringing his wife on a busman's holiday after he revealed his day job was security guard at one of the other Rainbow camps. The couple had two teenage children, but the youngsters almost always skidded into the dining hall behind everyone else, pulling out their chairs while mumbling apologies to their mum and dad. The family were having a fantastic time, and Liz thankfully fell into conversation with the parents, totally focusing her attention on them.

She congratulated herself on arriving

and taking her seat without knowing whether Rob was already in his or not. The two teenagers arrived within minutes.

'Wonder what's for dinner,' said the boy, pulling out his chair.

'I imagine Liz here knows,' said his dad. 'If it's Wednesday it must be — '

'Steak pie, new potatoes and vegetables,' said Liz, on autopilot. The menu rotated the dishes according to the day of the week.

Liz knew Rob's favourite meal was the Wednesday steak pie with all the trimmings. As the soup plates were cleared and the waiting staff began bringing in the main course, she couldn't help but sneak a look across the aisle towards his usual seat. At once she caught his eye.

Okay, so he'd been gazing at her — or he'd been playing the same game and they'd caught one another out. She looked down at her plate and wished her heartbeat would stop its gallop and slow to normal pace. It hadn't helped when, earlier, Angie chose to play 'I Can't Stop Loving You'. All of a sudden the whole thing seemed too funny for words. Liz tried hard to suppress a smile but found it far too difficult.

Fortunately one of the men sitting opposite the security guard began telling groan-inducing jokes aimed at trying to make the teenagers crack a smile. He had little success, but Liz made up for their disdain and extreme eye-rolling by laughing easily, no one else aware she was trying to rid herself of pent-up emotions.

Next time she glanced in Rob's direction, she didn't look away. He was nodding, focusing all his attention on the person seated on his right. Sadly he seemed to have lost his appetite, and Liz caught her breath as she saw him raise his forkful of succulent steak pie to his mouth and lower the fork again without touching the food.

And then in one of those precious cinematic moments you see on screen but are not often rewarded by seeing in real life, it seemed to Liz as if time stood still; as if there was no one else in the room, even the world, except Rob and her. Their eyes met. Neither of them looked away. She felt her lips tremble and she gave Rob the tiniest of nods, as if to say, 'Can we not stop torturing ourselves?'

In his turn, he smiled at her. It was such a sweet smile, full of understanding. And though her eyes were misted with unshed tears, she knew the tenderness was back. This time she returned his smile, and he nodded at her.

'Liz, what's tonight's play like? Would the children like it, d'you think?'

She looked away from Rob to answer the query from the teenagers' mum. When she looked back again, Rob was eating with every sign of enjoyment. But her desire for food had gone. She could only finish half her meal before putting down her cutlery. Where did they go from here?

'Hey, young lady,' said the holidaying

security guard, glancing at her plate. 'Lost your appetite? You must be in love!'

★ ★ ★

'What a pickle.'

'You could say that,' said Liz.

'So neither of you got off your high horse when you left the dining hall?' Jenny, her evening shift finished, looked enquiringly at her chalet mate.

'Rob left as soon as he finished his pudding. I was in the middle of a conversation, so it would've been rude to jump up and run after him.'

'Would you truly have made the first overture, Liz?'

Liz considered. 'Oh dear. If I'm honest, I want him to be the one who does that, even though I've thought things through. There are always two sides to an argument; but it still hurts, knowing he was so swift to believe the worst.'

Jenny reached for a bar of chocolate

from her drawer and broke it in half. 'You'd better not have brushed your teeth yet,' she warned as she offered Liz the treat.

'I haven't. I didn't feel ready to try sleeping. Thanks, Jenny.'

'You can do the honours next time. You can probably do with something sweet.'

'I couldn't eat much dinner. Missed pudding completely, even though it was trifle, which I normally love.'

'Trifle.' Jenny broke off another square of milk chocolate. 'It's a mixture of different ingredients, combining to create something satisfying and delicious.'

'What are you trying to say?' Bewildered, Liz shook her head. 'My brain's not working properly.'

'I'm saying trifle's rather like a relationship, whether it's a romantic or platonic one.'

'A platonic trifle?' Liz laughed.

'I'll ignore that,' said Jenny. 'All relationships, like trifle, have several different requirements in order to work properly. One ingredient on its own may not be half as nice without one of the others to complement it.'

'Sponge cake, jam, jelly, fruit, custard, cream, plus hundreds and thousands on top of the trifle if you're my young brother!'

'There you have it. But some people would prefer to add sherry to that recipe. They'd also have their own ideas about which fruit to use in order to create the perfect trifle.'

'Come on then, Miss Agony Aunt, what's lacking in my relationship — or maybe I should say my former relationship — with Rob?' Liz leaned back against her pillow and hastily plucked a fragment of chocolate from the counterpane.

'It's not for me to say. Fortunately for you, I haven't accompanied the pair of you on your dates. But I'd say you both lack tolerance towards each other. If I'd been in your place, I'd have sat down and written a letter to Rob explaining exactly who Mike was and why you were so preoccupied with him.'

'A letter!'

'Yep. You could have given it to me or Colin or Angie to hand to him.'

'If you say so. It's just occurred to me that I wrote my letter of resignation to Stuart and I can't remember what happened to it.'

'When did you last have it?'

'I wrote it this afternoon, at the office. When I took it along to Stuart, intending to speak to him about my resignation, he gave me a very frosty reception.'

'What, do you mean before he knew you were handing in your notice?'

'That's right. He seemed in a dreadful mood, and when he told me he was dangerously close to losing a valued staff member, my heart dropped to my boots.'

'You don't mean Rob? Surely he doesn't want to quit his job too?'

Liz nodded. 'That's the impression I got from Stuart. Rob obviously feels as I do, but he must have got to the boss before I did. It's awful, isn't it?'

Jenny began changing into pyjamas. 'It's downright crazy, Liz. Neither of you wants to leave. You really must sort things out.'

'Angie gave me a tough time too. Apart from anything else, it's embarrassing knowing everyone's aware Rob and I have had a row.'

'I hope whoever made mischief for you with Rob is feeling ashamed of themselves.'

'Maybe they don't realise how much trouble they've caused.'

'And maybe they never will, if you get a move on and put things right. Are you sure you won't let me go to Rob and explain it's really me who's at the centre of all this?'

Liz got out of bed. 'I have to clean my teeth. No, Jenny, it's kind of you to offer but I really do feel it's down to me to explain the whole situation. That is, if he ever allows me to speak to him again.'

Jenny gave Liz a quick hug. 'I'll come with you to the ablutions, then we can get our heads down. This time tomorrow, all this unpleasantness will be over and done with.'

'Rob and I smiled at one another earlier. In the dining hall.'

'There you are, then. I wouldn't mind betting he's as miserable as you are, and feeling guilty about the way he's handled things. You mark my words.'

★ ★ ★

Liz arrived at her office five minutes earlier than normal. She hadn't seen Rob at breakfast and she wanted to be around in case he called on Stuart first thing, as he sometimes did. Stuart liked to be kept posted regarding the atmosphere in the ballroom as the hands on the big clock drew closer to eleven o'clock, when all good campers should head back to their chalets. Sometimes Friday nights were a bit rowdier than usual; but with so many families holidaying, often bringing grandparents too, the mood was mainly light-hearted.

Today, however, although Liz chose to catch up with her filing and stood facing her glass partition, the chief Rainbow host didn't turn up. When Stuart appeared in her doorway and informed her he wanted to dictate some letters and memos, she returned his morning greeting, picked up her notebook and pencils, and followed him to his office. They took their seats and her boss looked at her, a serious expression on his face.

'There's a change to the schedule you typed, Liz. I'm taking over Rob's duties tomorrow. That's why I want to get this dictation out of the way.'

'Is he all right? He's not ill, is he?'

'He asked if he could change his day off, and I thought it best to help him by standing in for him.' Stuart treated her to a rather wintry smile. 'I like to keep my hand in, though the campers will probably be disappointed when I turn up in uniform instead of Rob.'

Liz wasn't sure what to say. 'If — if this has anything to do with the disagreement between me and Rob, I'm so very sorry if it's causing you problems. This is why I decided to hand in my notice.'

Stuart began to cough and splutter while she spoke. He reached for the glass of water he always liked to have on his desk. 'I'm so sorry. Now, we'd better get on.'

Liz thought it best to co-operate and ride out the day, although she guessed it would be sheer torture not knowing what Rob was doing, and being unable to talk to him as she'd planned. She didn't want to visit Angie while the same standoff existed; and with all he had on his plate, she daren't ask Stuart if he'd come across the letter she'd written to him and lost.

The advantages of having a busy schedule when fighting one's emotions became apparent to Liz as the day progressed. She bumped into Jenny while on her way to collect the post, and her friend reminded her of her rendezvous with Mike the next day.

'Goodness, that's come round quickly. I'm so sorry, Jenny, but I was so wrapped in my own problems, I clean forgot about tomorrow.'

'Don't worry, Liz. He gets into town quite late this evening, so we're meeting at his hotel for breakfast tomorrow. He's booked in at The Grand — it's really smart, so I'm going to be out of bed early, dolling up!'

'Early night tonight then?'

'That's one of the lovely things about Stuart. The schedule never has any host or hostess on ballroom duty the night before their day off, so if anyone wants to leave before the evening meal, they're able to. In my case, I shall be beautifying myself after supper.'

'I'll give you a manicure if you like. I'm not doing anything special this evening.'

'That would be lovely. Thanks, Liz.' Jenny hesitated. 'Rob told me last night that he wouldn't be around tomorrow. Said he had some business to sort out and Stuart would take over his duties.'

'You can imagine how I feel,' said Liz.

'Well, I have no idea what's going on, but promise me you won't hand in your notice.'

'If I knew it would stop Rob from doing something silly, I'd do it in a flash. So far, Stuart hasn't been very communicative.'

'Hmm, no comment. Now, I must go or Colin will be sending out a search party. Have a good day, and don't worry.'

Liz watched her friend hurry across the concourse towards the children's playground. Telling her not to worry was all very well, but this uncertainty hung over Liz like a heavy black cloud, and she felt there was no one to blame but herself.

* * *

Driving to the Seacliffe Rainbow Camp, Rob reflected on the situation that he knew had escalated to a point where something, or someone, had to give. Stuart had readily agreed that he should swap his day off, even though it meant the entertainments manager putting on his blue-and-whites and jumping into the schedule for several hours. That was what all managers should be capable of doing, even years after swapping their colourful uniform for a grey suit, he'd told Rob. Take note!

Seacliffe was around seventy miles along the coast from South Bay, and Rob knew it was a very different holiday place from the one he worked at. Seacliffe attracted more young people; but as with all the Rainbow camps, there were strict boundaries regarding holidaymakers under the age of twenty-one. From what he'd heard, Rob knew that the type of entertainer booked as a special attraction differed from the more family-orientated type of performer Stuart favoured for his camp.

He arrived at the gate control and wound his window down. 'Rob Douglas from South Bay, to see your entertainments manager.'

The security guard consulted his clipboard and ticked a name. 'Right, mate. Wait for the barrier to lift and drive into the staff car park. Follow the road to your right and you'll find it, behind the reception building.'

'Many thanks.' Rob put the car into gear. He felt a sudden pang, recalling the first driving lesson he'd given Liz. Would she feel sad about being unable to continue with them? He hoped she'd stay in her post and maybe, just maybe, if things went his way, he'd be able to help her in the future. Just now he had an interview to attend. Rob put thoughts of Liz out of his head and manoeuvred his car into the first convenient space.

He knew that the layout of all Rainbow camps was identical, so it was second nature to walk towards the entertainments office. He kept his eye open for his opposite number, Graham, whom he'd met on a training course a while back; but although there were plenty of Rainbow hosts and hostesses going about their routines, there was no sign of him. Rob glanced at his watch as he saw the building ahead of him and quickened his pace. He took the stairs up from the coffee shop two at a time, and stood gazing at the familiar sight of a radio studio with adjoining offices. He tapped on the first office door and waited.

The woman not using the telephone came over and opened the door. 'Good morning, how can I help you?'

'I have an appointment with Ricky Martin,' said Rob.

'You're bang on time. I'll just make sure he's free.'

As soon as Rob was shown into the manager's office, he felt a wave of something that wasn't hostility by any means, but something was nagging at his consciousness. He'd better concentrate and stop imagining things.

'Rob, good to meet you,' said Ricky Martin, rising and holding out his hand. His eyes, Rob noted, were calculating, although his smile was wide. 'Now, take a seat. Can we offer you a cup of coffee?'

'If it's no trouble, that would be great.'

Ricky picked up his phone. 'I have the luxury of a secretary and a trainee,' he said as he waited for a response.

Rob smiled politely and wondered how he had managed to swing that. Stuart maybe wasn't shouting loud enough for another staff member or two. If Liz had an assistant, she'd be free to help out in the field, even though her secretarial qualifications were what had got her the job in the first place. Stuart had taken a chance and offered her employment on the strength of her CV and one brief phone call. Yes, the man had been desperate for assistance, but he must have thanked his lucky stars when Liz fitted in so well. Now, with that situation in danger of disintegrating, it was up to Rob to back off and see if he could convince Ricky Martin this role exchange between Graham and himself would be beneficial.

Half an hour and two cups of coffee later, the two men shook hands.

'Changeover Saturday then, Rob. You'll find Graham at the theatre now. He finishes judging a kiddies' talent contest at noon, so the two of you can have a chat then.'

'Thanks, Ricky. This is a good chance for Graham to add to his experience, and also for me to work at a camp with a different style from the one I'm used to.'

Ricky flashed a smile. It still didn't reach his eyes. 'I shall look forward to finding out what you think of us, Rob.'

'I'm not here to judge anyone, Ricky. I bow to your years of experience.'

Ricky hesitated before speaking. 'With regard to the minor problem Stuart mentioned, instinct and experience prompt me to ask whether this could influence the way you conduct yourself while working in my team. I hope you don't mind my asking.'

Rob clenched his fists at his sides. What was Ricky getting at? 'Ricky, please believe me when I tell you Stuart would not have recommended me for secondment if there'd been any major difficulty. As I mentioned earlier, there was a small matter of staff discipline, and somewhere along the line I got the wrong end of the stick. The other employee found it difficult to deal with things and that's all there is to it.'

Ricky nodded. 'Just checking. Stuart did say he thought a cooling-off period would help both parties. I'm very glad to help.'

Rob rose. 'I won't take up any more of your time. And I'll present myself at noon on Saturday.'

'Excellent.' Ricky opened the folder on the desk before him. 'Remind Graham to leave his chalet key with my secretary. I imagine you'll do the same at your end.'

11

Gonna Get Along Without You Now

On Saturday morning, Liz went to work burdened by a cold lump of disappointment inside her. She should be in a good mood, surely. The man who'd caused her to travel from anger through guilty tears to sadness, all laced with the emotional pull he possessed over her feelings, was leaving for his month's job exchange. This would put an end to the treacherous stomach-lurching she experienced whenever she came face to face with him. Rob wouldn't be around to generate any of this.

Stuart had gently warned her the chief Rainbow host would call in to leave his chalet key and update her of anything he'd thought of which he felt Graham should know. In addition, Stuart had finally convinced head office of the need to take on additional help in the office. Liz knew that once she had a helper able to take over routine tasks like collecting the mail and doing the filing, she'd have more time to help her boss with other responsibilities. And, although it could be a bit terrifying working at the sharp end, she'd be able to help out with hostess duties more often than at present.

Liz tried her hardest not to look across to Rob's table at breakfast that morning. And when she left the dining hall there was still no sign of him. She hurried along the concourse and pushed open the swing doors to the café, heading straight upstairs.

A tall figure stood at the top of the staircase, startling her when she reached the halfway point. 'Sorry, Liz, I didn't mean to give you a heart attack,' said Rob.

If he only knew what a devastating effect he had upon her heart! She climbed the last few stairs quickly. 'Good morning. It seems strange to see you here wearing civvies.'

'I skipped breakfast. Thought it best to fold my tent and get off a bit early. I can always stop at a café on the way.'

'I hope I haven't kept you waiting,' she said politely, unlocking her office. 'Is Stuart in?'

'I don't think so.' Rob followed her inside and closed the door. He held out his hand to give her his chalet key. 'As instructed,' he said. 'I think you'll get on well with Graham. He's a good bloke.'

Liz's heart reacted by telling her it was being slowly squeezed. 'Oh, Rob. I am so, so sorry about all this.' She turned away and placed the key in her desk drawer.

'No, it's me who needs to apologise, not you, Liz.' He stepped close enough to reach out to her and take both her hands in his. For moments they stood gazing at one another.

'Jenny explained the whole situation to me last night,' he said.

'What!'

'No, don't be cross with her, please. I wormed the truth out of her — all the stuff about her old boyfriend and how he turned up and spotted you in the ballroom. You and Mike knew each other years ago, so how could you not become involved when he asked for your help? I'm glad Jenny told me, but I'd already decided to come here this morning and tell you how sorry I am, without even hearing the story.'

'I see. Well, no, I shan't be cross with her.' A little smile forced its way out. 'I hope I'm not that much of a dragon.'

'Liz, I . . . Oh, what the heck. I can't bear to leave you without telling you how I feel!'

She gasped as he swept her into his arms and held her close, nuzzling his face in her hair, murmuring words of love, such beautiful words that tears sparked in her eyes.

'Don't go. Please don't go, Rob. I'll tell Stuart all this was my fault. We can be friends again, can't we?'

'I'm not sure we can.' He held her

even closer. 'Because I know I love you, Liz. It's been hell these past few days, trying to keep my distance, but I agree with Stuart — this separation is for the best. A month will soon pass, and by the time I return I hope both of us will know how we feel about each other. How we face the future.'

She tilted her face, looking up at him. 'All those lovely things you said just now, Rob. About being sorry for hurting me and wanting to make it up to me — '

'Uh-huh?' he said, bending his head so his mouth was temptingly close to hers.

'Did you really mean them?'

He touched his lips to her forehead, then touched the tip of her nose with his lips and murmured something unintelligible, but she knew what would happen and she wasn't disappointed. The kiss, that wondrous first kiss, the lack of which romantic essential Jenny had questioned, happened in the unlikely company of Liz's desk, typewriter and filing cabinet. But even without a canopy of silvery moonlight or a perfect sunset stroll along the sands, she was in a blissful state. Liz closed her eyes and breathed in the fresh morning scent of him. How delicious was the combination of peppermint toothpaste and lemony aftershave! The kiss continued a long, long time.

'I can't believe I just did that.' Rob drew back, still holding her gently.

'I'm very glad you did. I rather like feeling breathless.'

He groaned. 'I need to go, darling girl. Straight away! Or else I'll lose all my willpower, forget common sense, and cause too many people problems.'

'I know you have to go. I'll still be here when you get back, don't forget.'

'Promise?'

'I promise.'

'And you promise not to fall in love with Graham?'

'Don't be silly. And you'd better not fall in love with Ricky Martin's secretary.'

'She's at least forty years old, and a bit forbidding.'

'Don't be so rude. I hope she keeps you in order.'

'Hmm.' His eyes sparkled. 'Her assistant seems nice though, and she hasn't seen me in uniform yet.'

'Is that so? Well, Mr Douglas, before you go to your new fan club, I need to say I love you,' said Liz. 'In or out of uniform.'

'Whoa, Miss Lane,' he said. 'Maybe you'd better rephrase that comment!'

His expression spoke more than any words could have done. But with one quick hug and one swift kiss on the lips, he was gone.

Liz dabbed her eyes, blew her nose and peered at her reflection in her handbag mirror. She needed to make sure she looked neat and tidy before checking whether Stuart had arrived. She'd lost all sense of time and place while Rob was kissing her, and if her boss had glanced through the glass partition on his way to his desk, he might have got a shock. But oh how lovely, how incredibly wonderful it was to have made it up with Rob.

She was going to miss him so, so much. But he was absolutely right to stick to his original plan. Four weeks apart would give them time to think and consider their options. She had no contract with the company and would have no job at the end of September, whereas Rob was a permanent member of staff. She decided not to linger over such thoughts and get on with life, work hard and look forward to the day when he came back to her.

* * *

The morning flew by, what with one thing and another. Graham, Rob's counterpart at Seacliffe, arrived and was closeted with Stuart for an hour or so. In her office, Liz soon realised, much to her relief, that Susie, the new staff member, was quick to learn and quite capable of handling telephone calls once she'd been shown the system and briefed as to who might be calling.

'All kinds of well-known people ring this office — you could even take a call from Mr Rainbow himself,' Liz told Susie as she hurried her off to the dining hall so she knew where to go for her lunch once she was working on her own.

'I shall mind my Ps and Qs, then! I already know this camp gets some great performers booked. I always keep an eye on the local paper because their reporter likes to get an interview when he can.'

'I never have time to read the paper,' said Liz. 'But I sometimes have to deal with someone's agent or manager and fix an appointment for an interview. Did you notice we had Jon Pertwee appearing last week?'

'I did.' Susie looked wistful. 'I sometimes feel like booking a week's holiday so I can see some shows.'

'You mightn't need to go to those lengths,' said Liz. 'I'll have a word with

Mr Boyd or his wife, and even though you don't live in, I'm sure you'll be allowed to go to a performance as long as there's a spare seat.'

Susie beamed at Liz. 'Thank you,' she said. 'Did you meet Jon Pertwee?'

'I had to collect him from reception and escort him to lunch. He was charming and full of interesting anecdotes,' said Liz. 'There's a separate small dining room for VIPs which I'll show you after we've eaten. If there wasn't, they'd be swamped by autograph-hunters if we took them into the big one!'

On her return with Susie to the office, Angie put her head round the door to meet the new girl. The radio presenter asked Liz for a word in private before she returned to relieve her stand-in.

Liz walked towards the studio with Angie. 'I think I know what this is about,' she said.

Angie paused outside her glass cage. 'I have a few spare minutes, and I'd like to apologise — if you're still speaking to me, that is.'

'Of course I am. There's no need to apologise, Angie.' Liz chuckled. 'Although it shook me when I realised how scary you could be.'

'It worked though, didn't it?' Angie gave her a quick hug. 'I'm so sorry if you found it upsetting, but Stuart and I had a serious discussion about how we could stop you from leaving. We decided the best way was to harden our hearts and shock you into reconsidering.'

'I'll never know how you found out before I even got the chance to hand in my letter of resignation, but I have a fair idea who's to blame.'

'As you've given me such a lovely smile, I imagine you're not displeased with that person.'

'You imagine right. I love my job; and to be honest, I was dreading going home with my tail between my legs, my mother saying 'I told you so' and Dad trying to keep the peace.'

'I wasn't trying to flatter you by saying what I did about doing a good job. It was tearing me apart being so cold and offhand with you, though.'

'Considering how well you fooled me, how about you audition for the next drama production? I bet you could give Elizabeth Taylor a run for her money.'

'Goodness, Liz, I'd die a death.' Angie laughed. 'The thought of acting in front of a crowd of people gives me the heebie jeebies.'

'This from the woman who broadcasts to thousands of holidaymakers most days of the week.' Liz smiled.

'That's totally different and you know it. The main thing is you're still here; and though Rob isn't, the next month will fly by, you mark my words.' She peered at Liz. 'Things are okay again between you two, I hope.'

'I think you could say that, yes.'

'You're turning a fetching shade of pink, Liz. That tells me I'm right, and I'm very pleased for you. Stuart will be pleased too — as long as you and Rob aren't planning to elope together when he returns.'

* * *

'I, erm, saw Liz and Rob in a clinch this morning,' Stuart said.

'It's a relief they've made it up. How did you come to witness them cuddling?' said his wife as they walked towards their car at six o'clock.

'He was in her office, but of course it was early when I went past.'

'Did they see you?'

'I doubt it. They were, as I said, otherwise occupied.'

Angie chuckled. 'I can imagine. I made a point of apologising for the way I lectured her. I expect you did the same?'

'Yes; and as soon as the new girl's got the hang of things, Liz knows she'll probably be doing a few hours on the schedule for at least a couple of days each week.'

'As long as she's happy to do so, love. She applied for a secretarial job, remember?'

'And a jolly good secretary she is.

No, I think Miss Liz Lane will be fine with abandoning her typewriter now and then. She seems to have enjoyed standing in for Jenny the other week.'

'Liz is good on the radio too. I have some time off owing me, don't forget, husband dear.'

He opened the passenger door for her. 'Talk to her so she can arrange the schedule.'

'Should I speak to Graham first? He's making up the schedule as from today. Does he know Liz sometimes helps out with events?'

'I didn't think to mention it, so why not wait until young what's-her-name's up to speed, then sort it out with Liz? She'll tell Graham when she's standing in for you. When I check the schedule before it's typed, if I can't spare my secretary, I'll soon say so.'

Angie got into the car, waiting while Stuart walked around to his side. 'You're chuffed to bits she's not leaving us, aren't you, love?'

'Yes, of course I am. Apart from

being able to delegate things, I get used to people.'

'I know you do.' She patted his arm. 'By the time Rob returns, the season will be more than half over. Decisions will need to be made. I'm wondering whether you'll be called to head office any time soon.'

He turned to her. 'That matter is very much on my mind. I was going to say something to you later.'

'Can't you say it now? Otherwise I'll have to wait at least fifteen minutes before we get home, and then Mum and the kids will be around.'

He turned to face her, taking hold of her hands. 'I have something to tell you, but it may not be something you want to hear, given we were wondering whether to house-hunt. After all, we do like this area.'

She sucked in her breath. 'I knew it! The company are relocating you, aren't they? Oh Stuart, what about the children's schooling? More importantly, what about my mum? She uprooted herself after all those years to live near us, and I doubt she'd want to stay here if we upped and went.'

He squeezed her hands before releasing them and preparing to drive off. 'Let's go home. It may be a rented property, but you've made it feel like home, Angie. Our home is wherever we are — you, me and the nippers.' He pulled out of the parking space and drove slowly towards the gates. 'Your mum would be welcome to move with us if that's what she wanted. But while we're driving back, just have a think about how well she's settled in. Think about little things she's said lately.'

Angie glanced at his profile. As usual, it was impassive. She watched him wave to the guard operating the gates for them. This was their fourth season at Seacliffe, and she still liked their lifestyle. But she knew the ways of the Rainbow organisation as well as Stuart did. However, she and he longed to own a place of their own.

They drove through the town, Stuart

taking the road leading to the small village where the company rented a cottage for them. Maybe this was, after all, the best time to move on, with the children so young. Angie did as her husband suggested and mentally listed the positive things she'd heard her mother say. Apart from being a hands-on granny, her mum belonged to the local gardening club and WI. She'd joined the nearby golf club and, Angie realised, lately had been dropping a particular man's name into conversations. These days Angie often heard what Tom thought about this, that and the other.

'I've just realised how right you are about my mum,' she said at last.

Stuart slowed for the sharp bend before turning down the lane leading to their place. He parked in the lay-by as usual. 'So I'm not exaggerating?'

'No,' said Angie. 'I wasn't thinking straight. It may be that Mum has already put down too many roots here.'

'Better not say anything yet. Is she staying to supper?'

'She knows she's welcome, especially when she's prepared it!'

Stuart chuckled. 'I'll run her home when she wants me to, and after the terrors are safely tucked up I'll tell you everything I know so far. But you're right about me having to take a trip to London. And when I do that, I think you should come too.'

'They won't want me tagging along, surely.'

He tapped the side of his nose. 'I'll explain it all later.'

'It's a good job I love you,' she said. 'Are you certain you don't have to go back to the camp after supper?'

'Because it's Graham's first night, you mean? No, Angie; if I trust people, I believe in showing them so. Graham's ready for promotion, as of course Rob is.'

'Okay. I'll try to be patient.'

12

What's the Use of Wond'rin'?

Angie's mum didn't accept the invitation to eat with her family. She said she was being collected at half-past seven and taken to the golf club to join a party of ladies celebrating the winning of a team trophy.

'Will you be getting a lift home, Mum, or do you want one of us to come and collect you later?' Angie posed the question as her mother gathered her things, ready to rush out the door to join her son-in-law, who was waiting in the car.

Angie was left open-mouthed as her mother called a cheerful, 'No thanks, darling. Tom will be at the club for a committee meeting, and he said he'd hang on afterwards and take me home.'

Stuart received this update of his

mother-in-law's social life when he returned. 'Ah,' he said, 'that would explain why she had her hair done this morning. And why she was prattling on about her new dress. I thought she seemed to be taking a lot of trouble over a girls' night out.'

Angie dished up buttery new potatoes to accompany boiled gammon and salad. 'I wonder what the combined ages of those girls is,' she said thoughtfully, putting a plate before each of her children.

'One hundred million million years!' Peter, the younger of the two terrors, called out helpfully.

'He's being silly, Mummy,' said Hannah, his elder sister.

Angie, who loved her children dearly and valued the time spent with them, couldn't help but feel relieved when Stuart took over bath time and pyjamas. He even read the bedtime story while Angie washed up. When she'd tidied the kitchen, after a moment's hesitation she decided a glass of something stronger than orange squash might be just the thing.

Stuart smiled as he joined her in the living room. 'You've opened a bottle of Blue Nun? Anyone would think we were celebrating!'

'Or drowning our sorrows? This is one I put by for a rainy day, but I thought the occasion deserved a little tipple.'

'If nothing else, we can celebrate the resolution of the Rob Douglas and Liz Lane dilemma!' Stuart picked up his wine.

'Cheers.' Angie chinked glasses with him. 'It's a great relief. But come on, Stuart, stop being so mysterious about your future.'

'Our future, you mean.'

'You're the main breadwinner, love. I can't expect to walk into another camp and take over as radio presenter, now can I?'

'No, but what I have to discuss with the head of entertainment is a position at a new hotel, not a holiday camp.'

'Are you serious? You can't mean that luxury one you were talking about before we started this season?'

'The very same. It's also on the south coast, but handy for Bournemouth, so it's in prime holiday territory.'

'But surely a hotel is very different from a holiday camp. How many guests would this new one cater for, compared to the huge number here when we have a full house?'

'A few hundred rather than a few thousand, yes, but everything will be scaled down and designed for the discerning holidaymaker. The aim will be to attract more couples, especially those who might be tempted by package tours to the Costa Brava. Because the cost would have to be more than what people pay for a week at a holiday camp, fewer families would be able to afford to stay. But I think it's very forward-looking.'

'Do you really? But what would it be like if you were in charge of the entertainment at this new hotel? Surely you wouldn't have so much to do?'

He sipped his wine and held the glass stem between his fingers. 'I'd be instrumental in drumming up conference trade as well as doing the kind of work I do here. There's a separate accommodation block being built where trade union delegates could stay — or teachers or whoever else needed a venue for a conference. The hotel staff would of course do the catering.'

'And what about staff accommodation?'

'Don't look so worried. There'll be a separate staff block and much better facilities than the camps can provide, I hasten to say. The new manager would be installed in a house offsite.'

'Just as well I opened this wine. There's a lot to think about. Tell me, have you actually been offered the manager's job?'

'Yes, but I've told them my answer's on hold, pending discussion. I'm flattered to be asked, but before I decide, I need to know what you think, Angie.'

'Thank you,' she said. 'Some men

would make up their mind without consulting their wives.'

He nodded. 'I only have one wife, so that saves a bit of trouble.'

Angie giggled. 'You know what I mean. But this does sound like an exciting opportunity, though it would scotch our plan to buy our own house, wouldn't it?'

'Not necessarily. I could probably come to some arrangement with the company. Whether they're purchasing or building a property for whoever's in overall charge, if the manager wanted to live in his own house they might be prepared to let the company property and make an income that way.'

'Without accommodation provided, you'd need a salary increase.'

'That's my girl.'

'Oh Stuart, how on earth do we decide what's best?'

'If I turn this down, I don't think it'll be held against me. You know I've always liked the idea of helping ordinary families enjoy a seaside holiday in

Britain. Especially without having to worry about keeping the kids happy on rainy days.'

'You'd have to wear a suit every day!'

He shrugged. 'Probably an evening suit for special functions.'

'Mmm, like Sean Connery in the Bond movies.' She sat up straight. 'Will there be Rainbow hosts and hostesses in uniform?'

'Definitely,' said Stuart. 'But I'm sorry to say there's no plan for a hotel radio station. Guests will come down to breakfast during normal hours without any wake-up call unless it's booked with reception. No first and second sittings. No music playing onsite like we have here. Any music will be arranged as a concert or dinner dance.'

'You know what I'm thinking, don't you?'

'Of course. It's one reason we're talking this through now. I'm sorry, Angie, but if I decide to take this opportunity, and if you really want to go on working for Rainbows, it won't involve the radio.'

'I think I'd enjoy reception work,' said Angie thoughtfully. 'But without my mother to help care for the children, I — '

'This is why we need to weigh up the pros and cons,' said Stuart.

★   ★   ★

As Liz strolled back to her chalet after watching a film, she remembered Jenny and wondered whether she'd still be awake when her friend returned from spending a day with Mike.

Jenny let herself in while Liz was listening to Radio Luxembourg on her portable radio. 'I wondered if you'd still be awake.' Jenny locked the door behind her.

Liz composed her features into as stern an expression as she could. 'You probably hoped I wouldn't be,' she said.

Jenny immediately looked guilty. 'Ah, I suppose you've discovered I sneaked on you to Rob. I'm sorry, Liz, but I couldn't bear to see you so unhappy.' She perched on her bed and gazed at Liz. 'Tell me you've decided to stay on!'

'Well, maybe I have, maybe I haven't.'

'Has Rob left? Did he apologise first? Have you two made up?'

'So many questions! Yes, he went to Seacliffe this morning, but not before he'd come to see me; and, well, each of us apologised to the other.'

'I suppose he couldn't very well not go, having got the job exchange sorted with Graham.'

'Indeed he couldn't. But we parted on good terms.'

Jenny pulled a face. 'Nothing more than that? Come on, Liz, haven't you got something exciting to tell me?'

'I'm not a girl to kiss and tell!'

'Aha! I knew it. So you two have had that first kiss. I'm so pleased for you. Will he come and see you on his day off?'

'No; he thinks we both need time

away from one another to consider the future, and I agree.'

'Do you mean what I think you mean?'

'I don't know. What would that be, then?'

'It sounds to me as though he wants you to be part of that future.'

'Driving lessons and all?' Liz propped herself on one elbow and switched off the radio. 'Yes, of course I hope that too, but I don't suppose it'll be easy. Now I'm longing to hear how you and Mike got on after all this time.' She yawned. 'Ooh, excuse me, but I'm so tired that I can hardly keep my eyes open.'

Jenny stood up. 'I'll get ready for bed, but I can tell you we had a super time. We walked on the beach after the biggest breakfast known to mankind. Then we took the bus out to that pretty village with the thatched cottages.'

'Wellworthy? It's where Rob took me for a meal on our first date.'

'The hotel is lovely, isn't it? We

skipped lunch because neither of us were hungry, so we had a delicious afternoon tea there instead.'

'Lots of nice food. But what about the really important question?'

Jenny scrambled to her feet and held out her left hand. 'I'm wearing Mike's grandma's engagement ring, and I couldn't be happier, Liz.'

She crossed the space between their beds and stooped so Liz could see the sparkling emerald, set in gold, with one small, perfect diamond nestling either side.

'He arrived with the ring in his pocket then? Yippee! It's gorgeous. Congratulations, Jenny. Give us a hug.'

'We should sleep well tonight, with all that's been happening today.'

'Most of my day was jolly hard work, but it began very delightfully.' Liz snuggled down again.

'I wouldn't mind betting you're asleep when I come back from those pesky ablutions. Wouldn't it be wonderful to have our own private bathroom?'

But Liz, already close to the land of nod, made no response.

$$\star \quad \star \quad \star$$

'Everyone seems to agree Graham's very pleasant and not quite such a slave-driver as Rob is.'

'Hiya, Harry, is that so?' Liz said with a laugh. 'Maybe he's letting everyone down gently for the first few days.'

'Maybe I'm reminding you there are other fish in the sea, sweetheart. Remember what I said before?'

She remembered. She also remembered what her reaction to his comment had been. 'I'm not interested in fishing, Harry. Although I suppose there are plenty of boats to hire down at the jetty.'

Harry stroked his chin, gazing thoughtfully at her. He'd shown her nothing but kindness since her arrival, but he so loved to gossip, and she didn't feel inclined to let slip any choice titbits of information.

'So is it on or is it off, Miss Lovely Liz Lane?'

'Do you mean my fishing trip?'

He laughed. 'You are a one. I hope that young fellow behaves himself and comes back to you, if that's what you want. And how about your chum, Jenny? How's her love life these days?'

'I couldn't possibly say, Harry. You can ask her yourself later. I seem to recall you're both hosting the beetle drive this afternoon.' Liz couldn't resist a sly smile. Once he saw that beautiful ring on Jenny's finger, he'd realise she'd been teasing him.

'You're a hard woman,' said Harry. 'But Rob's a lucky man if he still has a place in your affections.'

'We're friends again, Harry, but that's all you're going to get from me. I need to go back to work.'

'Friendship is something to be valued, sweetheart.' He began walking away. 'Now I too must go to my next port of call. A Rainbow's day is a long one.' He blew her a kiss.

She blew a kiss back. 'You can say that again,' she called.

There had been so much to think about lately. Falling out with Rob, wondering whether she should stop mooning over him as well as thinking of her future job prospects, and booking driving lessons while he was away. Wondering about Jenny and Mike — now a newly engaged couple with their own future to plan. They too faced separation in the autumn unless Jenny planned on finding a job somewhere near his college. She had time to think about it, even if everyone said the summer season was racing by.

Angie had seemed preoccupied when Liz spent a few minutes with her during their respective breaks. Liz hoped nothing was wrong with one of the children, or with Stuart. The Queen of Rainbow Radio's busy life was so different from the life Liz's mother led. Being a working mum was demanding, even though Angie's mum lived close enough to help out. Maybe Angie was suffering from the mid-season blues.

Liz ran up the flight of stairs leading to her office and almost collided with her boss. He greeted her with an unexpectedly wide smile.

'I'm just off to the barber's,' he said. 'I'll be back within the hour.'

'I should have your letters all ready for signing by then.'

'Excellent. And perhaps you could sit in with my wife for an hour when you're free. She's expecting you. We hope you can help out in the studio on Wednesday.'

'How long would it be for?'

'The morning's all settled, so just from lunchtime until before your evening meal.'

'You can't mean it! I'm still learning, Mr Boyd. What if I make some terrible mistake?'

'You'll be fine,' he said. 'Talk to Angie later.' With that, he clattered on his way downstairs.

But Liz couldn't wait to find out why she was needed for a radio shift on

Wednesday. She practically danced a jig outside the glass partition, waiting for the presenter to spin the next record.

Angie came to the door. 'Are you coming in now?'

'Not quite. I have a couple more letters to type, then Stuart wants me to sit in with you. Is something special happening on Wednesday? I hope everything's all right with you, Angie.'

'Everything's fine, but we have decisions to make. On Wednesday we're off to London for a meeting at head office, and I have Celia covering the morning hours, but the only other person up to the job is you, Liz. A little more time on air to build your confidence and you'll be fine.'

'I sincerely hope you and Stuart are right.'

'I'd bet on it. If you like, I'll ask Graham to call by. He's done quite a bit of radio work — but I doubt you'll need rescuing.'

'Could he not do the afternoon session, if we asked him nicely of course?'

'See you later.' Angie shut herself in again with a smile.

Goodness, this sudden need for decision-making must be catching. Liz, dismayed at the thought of the scary task ahead of her, wondered why she'd ever agreed to learn her way round all those knobs and switches in the first place. At least Rob wouldn't be around to hear her if she made a muddle of her announcements.

13

Mr Postman

My dear Liz,
This is the first chance I've had to sit down and write to you. I'm not very good at this letter business, even though I spent years away at boarding school and we had to write home every Sunday without fail. I'll try not to bore you, and at least I shan't be talking about the Saturday cricket match like I used to!

I hope Graham's enjoying his new base. I have mixed feelings about mine, but please don't tell him what I said. This site's not as spacious as ours, and of course it's a much older one, so the staff chalets especially are a bit battered. I'm working with a couple of people who I worked with in my first season as a very green

Rainbow even though I was dressed in blue! I wondered if they might be a bit resentful of me coming in here as the 'head boy', but they seem fine, thank goodness. I'm sure Graham's being made to feel welcome by all of you, too.

Liz put down the letter and thought. Rob was revealing something about himself she hadn't known. The mention of boarding school made her think his people might be well off. He'd had the use of his father's lovely car — what if she'd bumped into something and damaged the vehicle? She felt hot and cold at the very thought.

Rob spoke very well too, having no particular accent. It hadn't dawned on her before, what with all she had to think about. What if she and he were poles apart and attracted to one another for that reason? Her mum especially had disapproved of her daughter's new job. What might she make of a boyfriend who moved in very different circles from theirs?

She knew she was being silly and began reading again.

I've been thinking about your driving lessons, and I'm aware my father will need his car back soon. I'll probably be travelling back to South Bay by train when this stint's over, unless I can get a loan from Pa so I can buy something small and modest. That way you can continue your lessons without stumping up cash for a driving school course. Please don't protest, Liz. I could do with my own transport anyway. It goes without saying I hope you'll allow me to help you learn after I return.

I can't wait to hear how you're getting on, but only if you'd like to write to me.

With best wishes and much love,
Rob x

Liz read the letter through again with mixed feelings. Because this was the first love letter she'd ever received, she wasn't quite sure what to make of Rob's effort. But he admitted his own opinion of his letter-writing skills, and to be fair, he'd taken time out from his busy schedule to contact her. She would write back, of course, but she couldn't help thinking he'd set the tone for their correspondence. How much of her feelings she would transfer to the sheet of notepaper was not something she could easily decide upon. Too polite and formal and he'd wonder if she really did have a heart at all. Too loving and he might think she was becoming possessive. She'd just have to see how she felt in a few days' time when she replied to his letter.

* * *

'Staying in tonight, Liz? Wish I was!'

'You've changed since you came back from seeing Mike, do you realise that?'

Jenny nodded and picked up her hairbrush. 'I still enjoy my job, but I can't say I'm over the moon about ballroom duty these days.'

'I expect everything will get sorted out in time. That's what I try to tell myself, anyway.'

'Are you writing to Rob?'

Liz hesitated. 'That's the plan. He's already been gone a week, would you believe?'

'Golly, yes, you must be right. I'll drop Mike a line tomorrow. It's difficult to find a quiet half-hour these days. Good job he's so patient.'

'Now that you're engaged and you both feel secure about one another's feelings, it must be lovely for you.'

Jenny hesitated, hairbrush in hand. 'It is.' She cocked head to one side. 'I'd have thought with your letter writing skills, you'd enjoy using the kind of words that, well, no way would Stuart dictate in one of his memos!'

Liz laughed. 'Can you imagine? But the letter I really want to write to Rob might frighten the daylights out of him.'

'In what way?'

'Our relationship is nowhere near as stable as yours and Mike's. You two have shared history. Rob's and mine, well it's fragile, to say the least. That's why I'm wary of revealing how much I care for him. I may be able to streamline Stuart's dictation into shape, but I'm not sure I can make a good job of writing a love letter to Rob. Isn't that awful?'

'Understandable, I'd say. Has he written to you yet?'

'Yes, and it seems to me he was feeling the same as I am now. He talked about borrowing money from his father to buy a car, as if he needed something to help fill up the page.'

'But that's an important decision he's making. Why don't you start by telling him any news you have about the camp, and move on to telling him how difficult you're finding it to express your feelings for him?'

'I can do that with no trouble at all. What then?'

Jenny pointed the hairbrush handle at

Liz. 'Go for it. Tell him that when he comes back, you'll be able to say the words you really want to say to him. Make him aware how much you long to see him again, but without going into too much detail. Confide in him.'

'Goodness, I like the sound of that, Jen. Whatever would I do without you?'

Her friend slipped on her blue blazer and walked towards the door. 'If you feel like it, come and have a mug of hot chocolate with me when I finish.'

When she'd gone, Liz began writing, and to her surprise, she found the words came easily.

⋆　⋆　⋆

Rob called into the Rainbows rest room to check whether he had mail. To his disappointment, there was nothing but a slightly saucy seaside postcard from Colin, telling him everything was going well and wishing the same for Rob too. Colin was a great chap, but Rob longed to be ripping open Liz's first ever letter.

Maybe his letter to her had been delayed. He knew how busy she was, but surely she could spare time to write to him? He felt peeved, and reminded himself how his mother would scold him for being inconsiderate.

Rob headed towards the theatre, smiling to himself when he realised his feet were following the route without him having to think about it, as all the sites were built to the same plan. He unlocked the outer door, bounded across the foyer, and pushed open the set of swing doors leading to the stalls. Clutching his clipboard, he walked towards the stage. There would be two dozen hopefuls turning up for a preliminary audition that afternoon, and his partner hostess would be Rose. Rob screwed up his face in concentration. He knew she was one of the dancers from the resident troupe, but so far he hadn't worked with her.

He was sitting in the front row, thinking he'd arrived far too early and wondering whether Liz was thinking of him, when he heard the doors open and swing shut. He turned round in his seat and saw a woman in green and white making her way towards him.

Rob got to his feet at once. 'Hiya, Rose. Good to see you.' He moved into the central aisle and smiled as she descended the carpeted stairway.

She came closer. Her response was to stand on tiptoe in front of him. Next thing he knew, she was pulling his head down towards hers so he breathed in her sweet powdery perfume. Somehow he managed to avoid her mouth, so her lips landed on his left cheek.

'That's some greeting,' he said, keeping his distance.

'Obviously not as welcome as I hoped it would be,' she said. 'Should we try again?'

She took a step forward. Rob saw her purposeful expression and felt a moment of panic. Why the heck didn't someone turn up and rescue him from this ticklish situation?

No one did. But Rose began giggling

and at first he glared at her, annoyed by her obvious lack of concern over his discomfiture.

'Oh Rob, if only you could see your face,' she managed to say when she regained her composure. 'I tried to steal a kiss for a dare. You've made quite a hit with our dancing troupe, but the general verdict is you're a bit too terribly British!'

He tried his best to look aloof but realised he was playing right into Rose's hands. He knew he looked hunted, and that was only causing Rose more merriment. Her laughter was infectious, and the pair of them laughed so much that Rose gasped and said she'd got a stitch. She bent from the waist down while he stood by, feeling awkward and wondering whether to fetch the first-aid box.

A whistle and a catcall soon brought Rob to his senses. Contestants were arriving, and he hated anything less than professionalism within his job. 'Are you okay?' He peered anxiously at the pretty dancer.

She took a deep breath and nodded before turning to greet the holidaymakers. Rob's first thought was that he'd be the laughing stock of the Rainbows, but Rose didn't have a spiteful bone in her body. The two worked well together that afternoon; and as they left the theatre, Rose surprised him again.

'I didn't get around to asking earlier, but as part of my dare, the girls want me to ask if you'll have your photograph taken with all of us surrounding you. I'll never hear the end of it if you refuse, so how about it?'

'Put like that, how can I possibly say no? It's a deal.'

'We'll fix a time soon.' She glanced sideways at him. 'I suppose you already have a girlfriend?'

Without hesitation, Rob stopped and kissed Rose on the cheek. 'I do. Her name is Liz, and I'm hoping she'll marry me one day.'

* * *

Next day Rob received a letter from Liz. He collected it from Graham's pigeonhole and folded the pale blue envelope in half before tucking it in his inside breast pocket. He longed to rip it open straightaway, but he'd been waiting for this treat and intended to read the letter when he could find some peace and quiet.

With such a hectic schedule, he had to wait until lunchtime when he went back to Graham's single chalet for a break. Inside, he loosened his cornflower-blue tie and flung it aside before sitting in the one easy chair the company provided for its chief host.

At last he could open the envelope and see what Liz had to say. For a moment he worried she might have changed her mind, but told himself not to be so paranoid. To his delight, she'd included a photograph of herself that he gazed at before slowly relaxing in his chair, ready to read the words written so neatly in turquoise-blue ink.

Dearest Rob,

It was lovely to get your letter. You must have so much on your mind, and yet you're still thinking of my driving lessons. Yes, please, I would love you to continue teaching me, and not only because it's so convenient. I'm a little worried about you going to the expense of buying a car, but you do say you need one, so I hope your father will feel able to help you.

It's good to hear that the other Rainbows have accepted you, but I never doubted they would. Don't worry about Graham, either; he's very easy to get on with, but I don't think the girls and grans flock round him quite as much as they do round you! (I shouldn't really say that, and Jenny would kill me if she knew, but it's true.) Try not to break too many hearts while you're away.

Now comes the difficult part for me to write, but I've thought long and hard, so here we go.

Rob gulped. The words seemed to jump off the page and burrow inside his head. Was this where she told him she'd prefer it if they remained just good friends? He heaved a sigh and turned the sheet of notepaper over, dreading what he might read next.

Darling Rob, this is to tell you that I love you very much. It's true we haven't known each other for long, but we did begin a friendship, endured that awful falling-out, and, I hope you agree, emerged on the other side as more than just good friends. When you return, of course we have to go on working together and not show any affection while on duty. I can only imagine Stuart's reaction to anything like that! But when the season end is a little closer, I think I should look for a job locally, and some accommodation. If you don't like this idea, you can tell me, but I hope you agree that if we really don't want to be parted, come

September we shouldn't let each other go.

There! I've said it. Or rather written it. I hope you don't think I'm too forward, but you're very special to me and it's high time I told you so. I couldn't bear it when I thought I'd never see you again.

With all my love, dearest Rob.

Your Liz

PS: If you can send a photo of yourself, it would mean a lot to me. Colin took the enclosed snap the time I was standing in for Jenny, helping with the children. I hope you approve, despite my messy hair.

She hoped he approved! He was thrilled with it, and it would remain in his wallet now, hopefully forever. Rob looked down at the lovely laughing young woman waving in protest because Colin had snapped her with the breeze whipping her beautiful blonde hair around her face.

He held the letter next to his heart

and didn't tell himself not to be so stupid. Liz loved him. What was more, she'd paved the way towards a subject he needed to discuss with her. But that could wait until he returned and met with Stuart. And then he'd find the words.

14

There! I've Said It Again

'Botheration!' Liz clicked her tongue in annoyance as she tapped the wrong key. Try as she might, her fingers weren't doing what she intended them to do. At this rate, she'd still be wrestling with her workload when the first-sitting supper was announced. She forced herself to concentrate. She didn't want to be wading through pages of shorthand when Rob checked in after his four weeks away.

Ever since her boss and his wife had gone to London, there'd been a kind of aura about them. It was as if they shared a secret. Liz decided it couldn't be a happy event, because Angie had told her they were thrilled to have their two beautiful children but it would be unwise for her to risk adding to their family.

So what could it be? The only thing

Liz wondered might be a likelihood was a house purchase, given she knew the couple wanted to own their own property. But surely they wouldn't have gone to view houses in the London area. Liz typed on and on, eyes on her shorthand notebook. Two more memos after this letter and she'd be able to take the pile through to Stuart.

'Take a letter, Miss Lane!'

She'd been so intent on typing 'entertainments manager' instead of missing out the middle letter so it read 'manger', as she'd achieved on the last letter, that she hadn't noticed the tall man appear in her doorway.

'Oh my gosh, you're really here!' She stared at Rob, longing to jump up and into his arms but afraid to cause comment should anyone be passing.

'Oh no, you don't!' Rob approached purposefully and held out his arms. 'You didn't notice me walk past your window and go in to see Stuart, but I wanted special permission to say hello to his secretary.'

Liz rose at once, and Rob held her close before kissing her so thoroughly, so tenderly, that she thought she might collapse if he didn't keep his arms around her.

Too soon, he gently released her. 'I have to go in for debriefing now. But I'm told I have the evening off, as Colin and Harry are covering my normal Friday night duties. Please say you're not on schedule.'

'No, I'm free, Rob. Does that mean we can see each other later?'

'Just you try and escape.' He winked and headed out, pausing only to say, 'In case you're not here when I come out again, are you okay with skipping the evening meal? We could drive somewhere special to celebrate.'

'Celebrate your return?'

'Amongst other things.' His eyes twinkled. 'I have a new lady in my life. She's a little Ford saloon — but don't ask for a driving lesson tonight, lovely Liz, because we have other things to concern us.'

Liz, wearing a pink and white frock, made her way past the camp chapel to meet Rob.

'You look like Sandra Dee,' he said, walking towards her.

'Flatterer.' She snuggled against him as he drew her close and kissed the tip of her nose.

'Come on, let's go somewhere away from the hordes.'

'Without them, you'd be without a job,' she said, grabbing his hand. At once she remembered her decision to ask him whether he came, as she suspected, from a privileged background. It shouldn't matter, but she wanted to know.

He opened the passenger door, teasing her as she tidied her circular skirt, puffed out by a net petticoat, away from the gearbox.

'Where are you taking me?' She settled back as Rob joined her.

'Somewhere you like.'

'I wondered if you'd choose to go back there. Yes, I do like that hotel, Rob, but it's quite pricey. Though I get the feeling you're not exactly strapped for cash?'

'What makes you say that? You're right, as it happens. My grandfather left me a little fund.'

'I suspected it before, and when you mentioned your education in your first letter, I knew it must be true. It sounded as if you went to the kind of boarding school where only certain folk can afford to send their children.'

'Tuck boxes, cricket whites, church service on Sunday, and — ah yes, that weekly letter home to Ma and Pa. Sorry, honey.'

'Don't be sorry, Rob. None of us can help our background. I went to the local primary and passed the scholarship to the grammar school.'

'And what a fantastic job your folks made of your upbringing.' He squeezed her hand as he drove through the gates.

'Well, my dad earns good money, and

my mum hasn't gone out to work since before I came along. I can't remember a time when Dad didn't have a car.'

'That makes you posh,' he teased. 'How come he never taught you to drive?'

'I wasn't very interested,' she said. 'I played a lot of sport, but I also spent lots of time in the local library.'

'I never knew that.'

'There's a lot we don't know about each other, Rob Douglas.'

'It's fun finding out,' he said.

She sighed.

'What's that for?'

'It was a happy sigh.'

'Good. Now, after we reach the hotel, I want you to know that I have rather a lot to say. It's not how I'd have liked to arrange things, but because of the nature of my work — and yours, of course — certain matters need to be decided if you and I are going to go steady.'

'That sounds ominous.'

'It's not meant to be. But I'd prefer

to explain properly while we sit down and enjoy this beautiful evening together.'

Liz smiled to herself, looking at hedgerows alight with wildflowers. In the field they were passing, bright poppies made a red carpet, as though the month of July was determined to hang around as long as possible. That would be good. Liz was enjoying the moment, despite wondering what Rob might have to tell her.

*   *   *

At the hotel, a waiter took them straight through to the terrace, showing them to a table close to a white jasmine bush and with a view of the sea sparkling in the distance. While Liz sipped her favourite bubbly drink, Rob was half-way down his glass of lager.

'Come on then,' she said. 'Spill the beans.'

'Now you sound as if you're back in the 1940s.'

'That's one of my dad's favourite

expressions, and don't change the subject.'

'Okay. Firstly, I can't bear the thought of losing you at the end of this season. Darling, dare I hope you still feel the same?'

'You know I do.'

He gazed tenderly at her. The evening was a little sultry now, and Liz watched Rob run one finger around the inside of his shirt collar.

'What I'm about to say is partly due to information received from Stuart — and before you ask, I have his permission to tell you.'

Startled, Liz put down her glass. 'Information? This isn't bad news, I hope.'

He leaned across and tucked a stray blonde tendril behind her left ear. 'No, silly, this is information about future plans. So listen carefully, because you play a very big part in those — as long as you agree, that is.'

'Go on.' She held his gaze.

'Stuart has been offered an exciting

career opportunity. A promotion, in fact.'

'That's great news.' She felt a pang. 'So provided I'm accepted to come back next season, I'd be working for someone else?'

'Afraid so. Stuart and Angie plan to buy a house in the Bournemouth area, which is where the new Rainbows Hotel is being built. He'll remain as manager here until it's time to move on.'

'Does he know who'll be taking over from him?'

'Um, yes. But that person has very definite ideas about who he has in his team.'

She felt another pang of dismay. 'Are you trying to say you mightn't want to stay here? That you'll apply for a job in the new hotel so you can work with Stuart and Angie still?'

'No, I'm saying the person they've asked to take over from Stuart is sitting opposite you, Miss Liz Lane.'

She saw the seriousness of his expression and held her breath. 'But that's wonderful news, Rob. Oh my goodness, I'm so pleased for you.' She was on her feet and hugging him.

'Thank you,' he said when she was back in her chair. 'I'm very excited about it, of course. But would you be prepared to start the new season maybe working with Stuart for a while, then with me?'

Liz stared at him.

'You can think about it, of course. Take all the time you need. But I think we'd make a great team, just as Stuart and Angie do.' He hesitated. 'If you'd rather not put up with me in the office, Angie recommends you consider taking over Rainbow Radio after she leaves. You would, of course, be perfect for that position.'

'This is a lot to take in, Rob. I know I can't stay here in the off-season because there isn't the need for a full-time secretary. You know I wondered if I could find a job locally, but employers mightn't like the thought of me working for six months and then telling them I was coming back here.'

'True,' he said.

'I suppose I could go home and find a temporary job, and keep saving up until next spring.'

'So you'd still like to work here next year?'

'Yes, of course. I do love my job, crazy world as it is sometimes. But I don't think I'd like to be the full-time radio presenter, although it's lovely of Angie to think of it.' She paused. 'I can understand Stuart suggesting I work with you.'

'Sure thing. He knows I'll need someone who knows what she's doing.'

'Well, there's always Susie.' She shot him a mischievous glance.

'Hopefully we could ask her back too, as you'll still need part-time help. But this is about you and me, Liz. I don't want to spend the autumn and winter longing to be with you while Stuart continues training me.'

She frowned. 'I can't see a way round it.'

'Once you pass the driving test, you could apply for a job outside town. That'll give you a better chance of finding something suitable.'

'I hadn't thought of that, but I certainly won't be buying a car.'

'You could borrow mine.'

'Or I could take the train or bus.' She finished her drink. 'I'd need accommodation, of course. I've never asked, but where do you stay during the winter months? Surely those chalets must turn into ice houses?'

'The company has another property, don't forget.'

'You mean the house where visitors sometimes stay? I know Stuart says it saves a fortune on hotel bills.'

'Yep. That house is warm, it has five bedrooms, and I expect if you were willing to lend a hand at the weekend events, you could have a room there too.'

'My mother would be shocked to bits, Rob! I may be over twenty-one, but not in her eyes, I'm afraid.'

'So marry me.'

'Sorry?' She thought she couldn't possibly be hearing him right.

He leaned across the table and took her hands in his. 'Please say you'll be my wife, Liz. I love you, and if we become engaged, I'll come and meet your folks and reassure them we'll be chaperoned in the company house and that my intentions towards their daughter are strictly honourable. How's that?'

'I — I don't know what to say.'

'Do you want to be my wife?'

She nodded. 'You know I do. I love you, Rob.'

He chuckled. 'That's a relief.' He leaned across the table and clasped her hands. 'I love you, darling Liz. There, I've said it again.'

'I'll never, ever grow tired of hearing you say it.'

'Good. Because I fully intend to make sure we go on saying it for the rest of our lives.'

We do hope that you have enjoyed reading this large print book.

Did you know that all of our titles are available for purchase?

We publish a wide range of high quality large print books including:
**Romances, Mysteries, Classics
General Fiction
Non Fiction and Westerns**

Special interest titles available in large print are:
**The Little Oxford Dictionary
Music Book, Song Book
Hymn Book, Service Book**

Also available from us courtesy of Oxford University Press:
**Young Readers' Dictionary
(large print edition)
Young Readers' Thesaurus
(large print edition)**

For further information or a free brochure, please contact us at:
**Ulverscroft Large Print Books Ltd.,
The Green, Bradgate Road, Anstey,
Leicester, LE7 7FU, England.
Tel:** (00 44) 0116 236 4325
Fax: (00 44) 0116 234 0205

THE SCOTTISH DIAMOND

Helena Fairfax

When actress Lizzie Smith begins rehearsals for *Macbeth*, she's convinced the witches' spells are the cause of a run of terrible luck. Her bodyguard boyfriend, Léon, is offered the job of guarding the Scottish Diamond, a fabulous jewel from the country of Montverrier. But the diamond has a history of intrigue and bloody murder; and when Lizzie discovers she's being followed through the streets of Edinburgh, it seems her worst premonitions are about to come true . . .

PLANNING FOR LOVE

Sarah Purdue

Mia Bowman has a plan for everything. Right now, her plan is to go to Crete, leaving all family distractions behind, and finish her first novel. This is her dream, and she has its achievement scheduled down to the last minute. Then she meets the handsome Alex, and starts to wonder whether everything in life can be planned for. Soon, Mia must decide whether to stick to her schedule or follow her heart . . .

DANGEROUS ENCOUNTER

Susan Udy

After Kate Summers witnesses a violent stabbing, she finds herself running for her life. Along with her two children, she moves to a small Cornish town, where they live quietly and anonymously as they try to start afresh. Then Kate encounters the handsome Ross St. Clair, and her life begins to change again. When she senses danger once more, she knows she has to keep herself and her children safe from harm. But how?

THE HUSBAND AND HEIR

Valerie Holmes

1820: Major Buckleby seeks to marry his wilful eldest daughter, Charlotte, to his former captain, Mr Travis Williamson. However, she wishes to seek out a better match of her own choosing. Her younger sister, Rhea, wants to escape from Charlotte's temperamental outbursts, and is delighted when her father tells her that after the wedding they will travel to New South Wales. Travis is flattered by the proposition, but suspects there is more to it than he has been told . . .